## SHOOTOUT!

One of the gunmen farthest from him reached for his pistol. . . . All seven men exploded into action. Loud gunfire rang out. Gabe, with his rifle already in his hand, fired the first shot, putting a bullet into the stomach of the man closest to him. By the time Gabe levered another round into the chamber, the next gunman already had his pistol in his hand. He fired, too hurriedly, the bullet whistling past Gabe's head. Shooting from the hip, Gabe shot him twice through the body. . . .

# LONG RIDER

## ★ RANCHERO ★

## CLAY DAWSON

DIAMOND BOOKS, NEW YORK

This book is a Diamond original edition, and has never been previously published.

RANCHERO

A Diamond Book / published by arrangement with the author

PRINTING HISTORY
Diamond edition / December 1992

ISBN: 1-55773-831-9

Diamond Books are published by The Berkley Publishing Group,
200 Madison Avenue, New York, New York 10016.
The name "DIAMOND" and its logo are trademarks belonging to Charter Communications, Inc.

PRINTED IN THE UNITED STATES OF AMERICA

10   9   8   7   6   5   4   3   2   1

# CHAPTER ONE

The hilltop wasn't very high, but it gave a view. Gabe sat his horse quietly, studying the town that lay below. *El Pueblo de Nuestra Señora, La Reina de Los Angeles de Porciúncula*. That's what the Spanish had called it—The City of Our Lady, The Queen of the Angels of Porciúncula. Whatever Porciúncula was. A place? An old saint?

But the town was now called, by its new conquerors, simply Los Angeles. That fit a lot better. It wasn't much of a town, certainly not an impressive enough place to warrant that much longer moniker. From his vantage point, Gabe could see that Los Angeles was in a state of change, with new buildings going up everywhere. However, you could still see the bones of the old Spanish town showing through the patchy new flesh. Long low adobes existed side by side with modern buildings of several stories. New frame houses and false front businesses added their tawdriness. A plaza still existed, in front of the old Spanish church. An oval of small trees enclosed the plaza. All in all, it was a rather raw-looking town, although the frontier look was disappearing fast.

Gabe studied the largest building, a big brick and stone structure of three stories that took up most of one block. That had to be the Pico House. All the way across the Southwest, he'd been hearing about the Pico House. Built by one of California's former Spanish governors, Pío Pico, it was supposed to be the fanciest hotel south of San Francisco. Maybe he'd find out. Maybe he'd check in. He still had a sizable wad of his grandfather's money in his pocket; he'd spent very little on the trip west, sleeping under the stars, shooting or trapping a good portion of his food. Why not try a little of the White Man's luxury?

Gabe nudged his horse into movement and started down toward the town. No, not much of a place, but wonderful weather. Nice and warm. A fine bright sun shone down on the dry land below. And it was November. He could not help contrasting this land with his native ground—the plains of the Dakotas. He could imagine the icy winds that were now whistling across those vast spaces. But not here. November, and a warm sun. He could even see flowers below, bright little spots of color in someone's yard. Flowers, growing outside at this time of year!

He rode into town at an easy lope, a tall man on a big black stallion. He was dressed for the trail, wearing jeans, a denim shirt, a slouch hat. Long, sandy-colored hair trailed down over his shoulders, onto a stained linen duster. Not too different from many other men on the trail, except possibly for the long hair and the fact that he was wearing a pair of well-made Indian moccasins instead of boots.

He rode straight to the Pico House. It looked busy. A stagecoach and several buggies were tied to hitching posts in front. He tethered his horse and dismounted, shaking some of the stiffness from muscles that had spent too long in the saddle.

An arcade of arches ran around the hotel. Gabe walked through one of the arches, crossed the arcade, and entered the hotel, stepping into a big lobby. It was a fancy place, all right, with Turkish carpets on the polished floor, heavy furniture for lounging, and lots of dark, gleaming wood. He walked quickly across the lobby, toward the reception desk, and as he walked, his long linen duster blew open a little, revealing the butt of a big Remington revolver, worn on his right hip, butt forward, cavalry style. The reception clerk saw him coming, saw the revolver too, but made nothing of it. Los Angeles was a town where pistols were commonplace.

The clerk did notice the stranger's eyes, however. They were very pale gray in color, so pale that they seemed to have no color at all. Combined with his height, over six feet, and his long sandy hair, the eyes completed a picture that was guaranteed to attract attention. The clerk spent a couple of seconds sizing up the newcomer. Professionally. Which meant he wondered if this stranger had enough money to afford the Pico House.

Gabe's apparent confidence as he walked up to the desk reassured the clerk. "I'd like a room," Gabe said.

"With bath, sir?"

Gabe's eyebrows rose a little. A silent query. Most hotels had a bathroom, some more than one.

The clerk understood the unspoken question. "Most of our rooms on the second and third floors have private baths," he said smugly. "With hot and cold running water."

Gabe thought of the long, hot, dusty ride through the desert. Days of it. The thought of a hot bath, the chance to soak the dirt from his skin and loosen tired muscles, sounded damned good. "Yes," he replied. "A room with a bath."

The clerk nodded, then picked up a pen and asked Gabe his name.

"Conrad," Gabe replied. "Gabe Conrad."

"And who do you represent, Mr. Conrad?"

Gabe looked at the man bemusedly. So far, he had not met the clerk's eyes, which had made the clerk uneasy. He did not trust men who did not look him in the eye. But now Gabe looked straight at him, and the clerk became even more uneasy. Those light gray eyes seemed to bore a hole straight through him, and he felt a touch of instinctive fear. Then Gabe finally answered his question. "A lost cause," he replied softly.

The clerk wrote down nothing. He dropped his eyes from Gabe's and appraised his clothing. "I assume you are on horseback, sir. If you will describe the animal, we'll send out a hostler to take it to our stables. A room clerk will carry your belongings upstairs."

"Send the hostler," Gabe replied. "But I'll take the horse to the stables myself."

The clerk said nothing. Here in the West, the condition of a man's horse often meant the difference between life and death; the stranger's decision was not unusual.

Five minutes later, Gabe was walking beside a hostler who was leading his horse. The hostler had insisted, hoping he might get a nice tip if he did at least some of the work, although this tall, icy-eyed man walking next to him didn't look like he had a pot to piss in. They'd only gone a few yards when the hostler began to wish he'd let the man lead his own nag; it was a mean animal, and several times the hostler had to jerk his arm out of the way to keep the stallion from biting him.

They got to the stables without major incident, where Gabe supervised the unsaddling of his horse. The butts of two rifles protruded from saddle scabbards. He drew the rifles out himself, a Winchester Yellow Boy .44 caliber lever action, and a Sharps carbine. The hostler had already noticed the protruding butt of the pistol. This hombre's loaded for bear, he thought.

The horse was also carrying saddlebags and a bedroll. A room clerk arrived at the stables. Gabe gave him the saddlebags and bedroll to take to the room. "I'll carry the rifles," he said flatly.

But before he left the stables, Gabe made sure that the hostler had already started rubbing down his horse. The stallion was tractable enough now, he had his nose buried in a pile of hay. Gabe took one more quick look at the horse, making sure there were no visible physical problems, then followed the room clerk into the hotel, walking a few feet behind. Caution was so ingrained in him that he carried the Sharps in his left hand, the quicker-firing Winchester in his right, Instinctively ready for trouble without even being aware of it.

His room was on the third floor, which he liked; it gave him a view out over the plaza. After his gear had been placed on the floor, at his own request, he noticed that the clerk was still hanging around. He reminded himself of the White Man's endless thirst for money, then tipped the clerk a quarter, sending him away happy.

The room was large and ornately furnished. A big bed dominated one side of the room, a couch and two chairs another. A massive wardrobe waited for his clothes. But what interested Gabe most was a partly open doorway, through which he could see gleaming bath fixtures. He leaned his rifles against the bed, then stepped in through the bathroom doorway. A huge, claw-footed enamel tub stood against one wall. Thick towels hung from white enamel towel racks. A vision of paradise, like finding a watering hole at the end of a long, murderous desert trail.

Shiny taps with enamel handles jutted out of the wall over the tub. One was marked "Hot". Gabe turned it on and water rushed into the tub. He tested it with his hand. Cold. He'd thought so. The clerk's promises had sounded too good to be true.

He tested the water again. It was growing warmer. Within a few seconds it was too hot to touch. He let it continue rushing into the tub, then went into the other room to undress.

When he stripped off the calf-length duster, a sleek shoulder rig was revealed. The twin to the pistol on his hip lay snugly beneath his right arm, held inside a slim holster by a spring clip. A sheath had been sewn to the edge of the holster. It contained a long, thin-bladed knife, with the bone handle ready at hand. Gabe took off the shoulder rig, then his shirt, baring a lean, muscular chest, crisscrossed with old scars. The pants followed, taking the moccasins with them. A moment later he strode into the bathroom, naked.

He had to mix some cold water with the hot before he could get into the tub. His breath was sucked away by the heat of the water, but within a couple of minutes he had gotten used to it. He lay back in the tub, feeling tight muscles relax, seeing dirt float away from his skin.

Thick bars of soap lay close at hand. After ten minutes, he soaped himself thoroughly, then pulled the plug and let out the water. He rinsed himself with clean water from the taps, then toweled himself dry.

Stepping naked into the main room, he cast an interested glance at the big bed. A nap would be nice, but a loud growl from his stomach reminded him of other priorities. He picked up his shirt and saw how dirty it was. Same with his trousers, so he pulled his only other set of clothing out of his saddlebags and put them on, wrinkles and all. In a hotel this fancy, they should have a laundry service. He'd welcome getting his clothes washed.

He hesitated over the shoulder rig. Then he put it on, grateful for the reassuring weight of the revolver beneath his right armpit. He shrugged into the duster, and the revolver and knife disappeared from view. Hat and moccasins, and he was ready to eat.

He carried his dirty shirt and pants with him and gave them to a laundry woman on the next floor down. It was only about four-thirty when he got downstairs, but he could hear the cheering sound of cutlery and china from the big dining room. He wasn't going to go hungry.

An officious maître d' showed Gabe to a table. He sat down, amused by the snowy white table cloth. A damned sight cleaner and better ironed than his clothing. He looked around the dining room, noticing that about half the men eating were dressed little better than himself. There were several men in suits with vests. Businessmen, perhaps, or drummers, but Los Angeles was clearly a place in transition, and neither his clothing nor the pistol on his hip attracted undue notice.

Gabe ordered, asking for the biggest steak in the house. A cream soup came first, and while he was spooning it up, the dining room began to fill. He was about half finished with his soup when he became aware of someone approaching his table. He looked up. A portly man with thinning hair, wearing a rather gaudy checkered suit, was standing next to the chair on the far side of the table, one hand tentatively on the chair's back.

"The place seems to be full," the man said. "Mind if I sit?"

Gabe flicked a gaze over the man and instantly perceived weakness in his rather flabby face. Nevertheless, he nodded that the man could sit. Which he did. And once he sat, he never stopped talking.

His name was Sims. He didn't quite say it, but Gabe got the impression he was unemployed. "You're new in town, aren't you?" Sims asked for openers.

Within a few minutes, Gabe had Sims pegged. A grifter, gravitating toward a stranger in the fanciest place in town, to see if any crumbs might come his way. Sims immediately ordered a whiskey. After the drink came, Gabe watched veins flare in Sims's nose as he sucked the whiskey down.

Sims was a one-man booster for Los Angeles. "Growing like a weed, our fair city," he said pompously. "Wonderful investment opportunities."

Gabe nodded, certain that any investments Sims might recommend would fall straight into his own pockets. But he let the man talk. Gabe was indeed new in town, and perhaps this gabby stranger would tell him a few things that might be useful. So Gabe sat and listened, carefully averting his gaze, until he realized that Sims was getting nervous, and then he reminded himself that among the White Men you were expected to look a man straight in the eye to gain his respect. It had been so different among the Oglala, the People, where staring straight at someone was considered impolite, a threat, a challenge that might very well be taken up by the insulted recipient of that straight, unwavering gaze.

So Gabe paid close attention to Sims with his eyes. But Sims was still a little nervous. His eyes flicked around the table, came to rest on Gabe's mutilated right hand. The final joint of the index finger bent sharply away from the other fingers, at a ninety degree angle. Gabe saw where Sims was looking. "An old injury," Gabe said, partly to put the other man at ease.

"Guess that's why you're a lefty," Sims blurted out, pointing to the pistol on Gabe's right hip, holstered butt forward.

"Yes," Gabe replied, although he could draw quite well with his right hand, having practiced for many hours, determined to overcome the mutilation of his trigger finger.

The talk drifted back to Los Angeles. "Oh, sure," Sims said breezily, in reply to one of Gabe's infrequent questions, "Los Angeles still has its rough edges. There's the Pikes . . . drifters. And some bad apples come up from Sonora from time to time. Bandit types. And then, there's all those Southern sympathizers left over from the War. But all in all, this is a growing little metropolis. Of course," he said with a worldly laugh, "it might be a good idea to stay away from certain places."

"Such as?" Gabe asked. "*Calle de los Negroes*," Sims explained. "It's where the poorer Mexicans and some of the Chinese live. In Spanish it means Street of the Blacks, because some of them have dark skin."

Gabe remained silent as Sims continued to talk about the *Calle de los Negros*. "There *are* a few reasons for going there," he said, leering. "Women. Ladies of the night. Soiled doves. The cheaper variety. If you'd like me to take you there . . ."

By now Gabe was staring straight into Sims's eyes. Coldly. Sims was beginning to ruin his appetite, and a huge steak had just been set in front of Gabe. He could smell its juices, and his mouth watered. But he did not want to eat with this obnoxious windbag sitting at his table. Sims, fidgeting under Gabe's unwavering glare, finally got the message.

"Well," he harrumphed. "Business to attend to. I trust I'll be seeing you around town."

Gabe didn't bother to acknowledge Sims's departure. Instead, he tore into his steak. It was good. Not as good as the roasted buffalo hump he'd eaten in his mother's lodge when he was a boy, but good enough for a man who'd been living off jackrabbits for the past week.

A while later, stuffed, Gabe thought about that big bed upstairs. But he noticed through a window that there was still a little sunlight left. He decided to go outside and walk off some of his meal.

He stepped out into the street. Rich golden light struck the sides of the Pico House. The air was pleasantly cool, not cold. Gabe walked down toward the plaza, only about eighty yards away. He looked over at the old Spanish church. A strange gazebo-like structure crowned its bell tower. The little building looked rock-solid, immovable. Strange, how the White Men tried to capture their gods inside buildings.

As he wandered around town, he began to pay more attention to the people. He was surprised by the number of rough-looking men. Not many of them were what he would call hard men, but rather, small-time thugs. They swaggered as if they owned the streets. Maybe they did. He noticed a small family group step warily off the sidewalk to let three raggedly-dressed drunks pass by.

Not far from the Pico House, construction was under way on a large building. A sign said something about the Downey Block. Stores, businesses. Further out toward the edge of town, he passed more new construction. Vegetable fields were being plowed under to make way for the new buildings.

There were still quite a few of the old adobes left. Gabe admired their low, graceful styling. They looked cool and comfortable, looked as if they had sprung from the earth itself rather than being imposed upon the landscape. He sensed that few of them would last long. He remembered how Sims, at dinner, had talked endlessly about "progress". More and more people arriving, land being subdivided into smaller and smaller lots. All for sale. For profit. Progress? More like despoliation, the White Man's idea of growth, bigger and bigger, destroy the old. The idea of stability, of guarding what was old and good, was seen as stagnation. Grow or die. Like a swiftly spreading cancer, which, eventually, destroyed all around it that was healthy, good, meaningful. Progress. The White Man's disease.

He suddenly found himself in an older part of town. Here, things had not stayed the same; they had regressed. The buildings, mostly old Spanish adobes, had been let go. Unplastered, some were already crumbling. But they were not uninhabited. He saw a woman lounging in the doorway of one particularly run-down adobe. She saw him looking at her, and, smiling, she raised her skirt halfway up her legs.

This was the area Sims had told him about. Gabe looked over the woman. She was young and fairly attractive. He felt a slow stirring of desire. It had been a long time. But the woman was a prostitute, a low-class prostitute, and he did not want any of the White Man's social diseases.

The girl was still smiling. Then Gabe heard loud voices from further down the street. Two men staggered out of a doorway, both apparently drunk. The girl's smile vanished when she saw the men, and she disappeared back inside her doorway.

Both of the men were carrying pistols. And both were in a fighting mood. Gabe heard angry words being exchanged, which grew in virulence, until he knew that the men were going to fight. That did not bother him. It was a man's business to decide if he wanted to fight. It was what made a man a man. Too bad, though, that they had to ruin the cleanness of their decision by being drunk.

The final insult was hurled. "Why . . . you lily-livered skunk!" one of the men shouted, reaching for his pistol.

The other man was definitely not too lily-livered to reach for his own pistol. But he was too late, perhaps slowed by drink. He was still cocking his pistol when the other man fired. The bullet took him low in the chest. He staggered backward, his own pistol firing harmlessly into the ground. His opponent ran forward and fired again, at nearly point blank range, once in the stomach, once in the head. The wounded man dropped his pistol, then fell to the ground where he lay motionless.

Gabe walked down the street, passing not far from the dead man. The winner of the gunfight was standing over his opponent's body, mouthing obscenities. He looked up at Gabe, his eyes crazy, but something about the man passing by made him hold his tongue.

Gabe walked around the corner. A rough town, Los Angeles. He wondered what the law would do about the shooting. Would the law accept self-defense? A fair fight? Or would the law even take notice?

He was still wondering when he saw a small group of people walking toward him. The light was beginning to fail, and at first he noticed only that they looked strange. Then he saw that they were Chinese, a man, a woman, and two small children. Both the man and the woman had long hair hanging down behind their backs, braided into single pigtails. They wore long robes. The children were miniature variations of their parents.

The Chinese family was walking along hurriedly, heads down. Gabe saw why. Two men, of the variety he'd noticed earlier, street thugs, lounged against a wall, straight in the family's path.

The Chinese tried to go around the two men, by stepping down into the mire of the street. Gabe could see that it wasn't going to be that easy. Still forty yards away, he heard one of the men say, in a slow Southern drawl, "Looka that, Jethro. They let the monkeys out at night."

Jethro, a beer-bellied man probably in his thirties, snickered loudly. "I don't think they're s'posed ta be out, Harry. They're s'posed ta hide at night."

Both men stepped away from the building to block the family's path. Still looking down, the Chinese family tried to swerve around them. Harry reached out and grabbed the man by his pigtail, pulling his head back so abruptly that the man nearly fell. Harry held up the long length of braided hair.

"Yep." He snickered. "Monkeys. See? They got tails."

Jethro, meanwhile, had stopped the woman. But it was not her hair that he grabbed, it was her right breast. Gabe, who was now only a few yards away, could hear the woman give a little gasp of pain. "Goddamn!" Jethro said happily. "This one's got more'n a tail."

"I think you should let her go," Gabe said from directly behind Jethro. "They only want to pass."

Jethro spun around. Seeing the tall man with the pistol on his hip standing behind him made him hastily let go of the woman's breast. But by then Harry had turned, too.

"Who the hell are you, mister?" Jethro asked, encouraged by Harry's attention.

"No one in particular," Gabe replied. He looked off to one side, trying to keep everything polite. He did not want trouble his first evening in Los Angeles.

But, as with Sims, both Jethro and Harry took his lack of eye contact as lack of resolution. "You better get your ass outta here, mister," Harry snarled. "Ain't none o' your business."

Now he too turned toward the woman and began to paw at her. Her husband, white-faced, tried to get between her and the two men. Harry hit him in the face with his fist, knocking him to the ground.

"You stay there, goddamn it," Harry snarled, "or I'll put a bullet through your gut."

Gabe had already noticed that Harry had an old pistol stuck into his waistband. One of the Dragoon Colts left over from the Mexican war. A big pistol, rusted but apparently still functional.

Gabe stepped in close. "I said to leave them alone," he said in a harder voice. Harry spun and now found himself caught by Gabe's direct gaze. He took half a step backward, alarmed by the coldness, the lack of expression in those light gray eyes. But he was not about to back down in front of his crony. "Goddamn it, mister," he snarled, "I told you to . . ."

He made a half move for the old horse pistol. Gabe's move was faster. His fingers closed around the big revolver and tore it from Harry's waistband. Before Harry could react, Gabe smashed the pistol's heavy barrel across Harry's face. Blood gushed from Harry's nose. Crying out in pain, he staggered backward.

"Hey!" Jethro blurted. He was just to Gabe's right. Gabe backhanded him with the pistol, hitting him across the temple. Jethro dropped like a poleaxed steer.

Gabe looked at the Chinese family. They were clearly terrified. Anger bloomed inside him. What right did these two bullies have to threaten such harmless people? He took a step toward Harry, the big pistol still in his hand.

Harry, who had fallen back onto his rump, saw the look on Gabe's face. He'd seen a look like that once before, when he'd watched a man blow the head off another man with a shotgun.

"No!" he cried out, scuttling backward on the seat of his pants. "I didn't mean nothin', mister. We was just funnin' a little."

The rage inside Gabe continued to grow. The man was a coward. A coward and a bully. Gabe could understand a truly bad man. A coward, he could not. There was no one more despised among the People than a coward. The only thing to do with a coward was to kill him, not only for the sake of others, but for the sake of the coward, too. For how could a man continue to live, even want to live, once the world had become aware of his cowardice?

Gabe threw the old pistol away. He heard glass break somewhere. His right hand slipped inside the duster, came out holding the knife. Harry saw the gleam of the long, razor-sharp blade. With a little bleat of terror, he scooted away another few feet. Gabe kicked him in the face, knocking him over onto his back, stunning him. Before Harry could recover his senses, Gabe knelt down, grabbed him by the hair, and pulled him up onto his knees. Then he yanked his head back, baring his throat. The knife circled around Harry's body, ready to cut through his thick, dirty neck. Gabe tensed himself for the stroke, the rush of hot blood, the spasmodic jerking of Harry's body.

"No!"

Gabe looked up. It was not a voice he'd heard before. It was the Chinese man. His eyes pleaded with Gabe. "If kill him," the man said in thickly accented English, "very bad for us. Very, very bad."

Gabe froze, with the edge of the knife held lightly against Harry's throat. Harry had gotten his wits back again, but was too scared to move. Gabe looked into the Chinese man's face, was convinced by the worry and fear the man so obviously felt, not only for himself, not only for his family, but probably for all the other Chinese people in Los Angeles as well. Gabe understood. He was acquainted with the White Man's racism. Too well acquainted.

He abruptly stood up. The knife slipped back out of sight. Harry, still frozen in place, gingerly felt his neck. Gabe motioned the Chinese family away. They disappeared down the street, their long robes masking the quick movements of their legs.

Gabe kicked Harry in the side. Harry looked up, flinched as he met Gabe's eyes. "If you touch them, bother them in any way," Gabe said quietly, but with a sense of menace that Harry would not be able to miss, "I'll find you. Then we'll finish this the way it should have been finished tonight."

He walked away, too contemptuous of Harry to bother guarding his back. He felt anger still working inside him as he went into the hotel and headed up the stairs toward his room. His stay in Los Angeles had not started off well.

# CHAPTER TWO

Bacon, eggs, coffee, biscuits with gravy—Gabe could see he was going to get fat if he continued staying at the Pico House. He was packing away a workingman's breakfast, served in the big dining room. Other breakfasts were available. He watched a man wash down oysters and scrambled eggs with champagne.

After only one day, the good life was beginning to tire Gabe. He had not slept well. The big bed in his room had proved much too soft for a man accustomed to sleeping along the trail. He'd wrestled the mattress down onto the floor. It had helped a little, but not much. He supposed he'd get used to it in time, but he had no intention of staying in the hotel very long. Or in Los Angeles. He'd like to see the ocean; that was one of the main reasons he'd headed west. He'd seen the Atlantic before, now he wanted to ride beside the Pacific. Maybe another day or two here, then . . .

He looked up. Two drummers were eating not far away. He heard one snicker, then say, "Here comes one hell of a relic out of the past."

Gabe followed the drummer's amused eyes. An older man, probably in his sixties, had just entered the dining room, but his age was not what had set off the drummer's amusement. Here indeed was a vision of the past, an old Spaniard, dressed in full Colonial splendor: long, skintight trousers, with silver conchos running down the outside of each leg; a high-necked shirt with ruffled sleeves; a short, embroidered vest; a short cape-like garment that swirled as he walked; and capping it all, a flat, black hat with a wide brim.

Gabe was intrigued too, but it was not the clothes that drew his attention. It was the old man's air of utter dignity as he strode into the room, his calm, self-assured manner. Gabe decided that he walked like an Oglala war chief. Gabe cast a quick look at the two drummers, at their flashy clothes and smug manners, and now it was his turn to smile. How trivial they looked in comparison to this old Spaniard.

Gabe looked back at the Spaniard. For just a moment their eyes met. Gabe nodded. The old man hesitated just a moment, then nodded back.

The old man seated himself. His eyes roamed the room. A dark-featured waiter was standing near one wall. Gabe had already noticed that the waiter did no more work than absolutely necessary, but when he looked up from whatever daydreams were dancing behind his vague expression and saw the old man, he came to life immediately, rushing over with a menu.

"Don Andres," he said in Spanish. "I did not see you come in."

"Do not let it worry you, Luis," the old man replied drily. "Bring my usual breakfast."

Don Andres's breakfast appeared with unusual speed— big, soft-looking, steaming tortillas, eggs scrambled with chili peppers and some kind of delicious-looking sauce, and an entire plate loaded with strips of grilled beef. Gabe watched as the old man smothered everything in even more chili sauce. Gabe's mouth watered. On his way across the Southwest, he'd slowly become addicted to Mexican food; indeed, he wondered if he'd ever again be able to live without it. What the hell was he doing eating in the Pico House, when he could be frying his tonsils in the Spanish section known as Sonoratown?

The old man looked up to see Gabe watching him. Gabe smiled. "*Huele sabrosa*," he said, referring to the delicious aroma drifting his way from the other man's table.

The Spaniard seemed a little surprised at being addressed in his own language. He looked at the remains of Gabe's biscuits and gravy, reduced to a heavy, greasy mess at the edge of his plate. "I'm sorry that I cannot say the same about your breakfast," he replied quietly, in the same language.

"If I had known your type of breakfast was available . . ."

"It is not. . . . to everyone. But I will say a word to Luis. . . ."

"That would please me very much," Gabe replied.

The entire conversation had been quite formal, partly because Gabe was not yet completely at ease in Spanish, but also because the old man's entire manner was formal. "*Perdóneme*," he said. "I have been rude. My name is Velasquez. Andres Velasquez, at your service."

"Gabe Conrad."

"You speak *Castiliano* very well," Don Andres said politely, although Gabe was painfully aware of his limitations in that language, which its native speakers seldom called Spanish. He saw that the old man was looking at him searchingly. "You are . . . an *Americano*?" he finally asked, puzzled by Gabe's appearance, not so much his color or physiognomy, but his manner.

"I . . . was raised among another culture," Gabe replied. "The Oglala."

The old man's eyebrows raised in a silent question.

"One of the Plains tribes," Gabe explained, suspecting that the old man probably knew little outside of California.

Then Don Andres saw Gabe's moccasins. "Ah!" he exclaimed. "*Indios*." For just a moment his eyes were hooded, then he seemed to accept. "You are a long way from home." The old man looked away for a moment. "As I am . . . in the very land where I was born."

"I'm familiar with that feeling," Gabe replied softly.

The old man looked at him again, more sharply this time, and now there was something more than politeness in his eyes. "Yes. I suspect that you are."

There seemed to be no more to say. Don Andres returned to his eggs, beef, and chili. Gabe took a long, revolted look at his biscuits and gravy and got up to leave, sending a small nod in Don Andres's direction. The old man nodded back.

Gabe spent the rest of the morning in the hotel stables, checking over his horse gear, ordering repairs from the hostler. Then he went up to his room to clean his guns. He had not fired his revolvers for some time. Quite possibly, the loads were bad. He removed the cylinders from both pistols, then, using a tool that looked like an especially sturdy corkscrew, he carefully pulled the loads from each chamber. With a pin, he cleaned out the nipples at the back of the cylinders, making sure nothing blocked them. He put the cylinders back into the revolver frames and reloaded them, first using his powder flask to measure an exact amount of powder. Then he placed a ball at the mouth of each chamber, using the loading lever hinged beneath the barrel to drive the balls solidly against the powder charge. He then put a cap of thick grease over the end of each chamber, to keep the flash from one chamber from igniting other chambers. Last, he put new caps on the nipples, pressing them into place, feeling the soft copper expand around the hard steel of the nipples, careful that none of the caps split, so that they might later fall off.

He took two more cylinders out of a pouch and reloaded them in the same manner. He always carried spare cylinders; reloading during a fight took too damned long.

Satisfied, he spun the cylinder of each pistol, to make sure none of the caps stuck out far enough to hang up the action. He twirled one of the pistols around a finger, testing its balance. Fine weapons. He liked Remingtons more than Colts because of their solid top-strap construction. The Colts tended to shake loose. These two pistols had saved his life many times.

Changing the load of the big Sharps rifle was easier; it was a breech-loader. He worked the lever beneath the trigger, and the breech block rose up, baring the firing chamber. He carefully lifted out the old paper cartridge, cleaned the action, ran an oily rag down the barrel, then picked a new cartridge out of his cartridge pouch. Like all the others in the pouch, he'd rolled it himself, first winding stiff paper around a dowel, to form an empty paper cylinder, then he'd put a bullet in the nose of the cylinder and packed the rest with a carefully measured load of powder. That was the tricky part, to make the powder loads consistent. If not, each shot would fly differently.

He put the cartridge inside the chamber, then closed the lever. The breech block dropped, its sharp rear edge shearing off part of the cartridge, baring the powder charge so that sparks from the cap would ignite it. The cap came last, fitted solidly onto its single big nipple. Gabe lowered the massive side hammer to its safety position, just short of the cap.

The Winchester was the easiest of all. Just lever the stubby rim-fire cartridges out of the magazine, oil the rifle lightly, and stuff the rounds back into the magazine, all fifteen of them. Not much for distance, the Winchester, with its light powder load, but it put out a lot of lead very quickly. It was his favorite weapon for defending himself within a hundred yards. Any further than that, and nothing could beat the Sharps. He'd once hit a man with the big carbine at seven hundred yards. The carbine meant a lot to him. It had been a gift, along with the pistols. A very special gift.

By now it was early afternoon, and Gabe was growing hungry. Putting the pistols back in their holsters, one on his hip, the other hidden beneath his right arm, he walked downstairs. He was heading for the front entrance when he saw Don Andres standing in the lobby, talking to another Spaniard, a man dressed more roughly than himself, but in the same general manner. Don Andres looked up and saw Gabe.

"Ah . . . Señor Conrad." The old man's eyes sparkled a little. He nodded toward the dining room. "On your way for more bread and gravy?"

Gabe smiled. "No. I was thinking of walking over to Sonoratown. Looking up some tamales."

Don Andres didn't quite smile, but almost. "Yes, you will find good food there." His eyes lit up even more. "There is a place . . . in an alley behind a store. If you walk down the street . . . But," he interjected, "Jorge can take you there. He has just told me he is hungry."

Don Andres turned to indicate the man standing beside him. "May I introduce Jorge Gonzalez, my *capataz*. What the Americanos call a foreman."

Gabe turned toward the other man, who gave him a quick little half bow. Not a bending of the neck indicating subservience, but a mark of respect among equals. Gabe returned the same gesture. When he straightened up, he studied Jorge for a moment, as Jorge was studying him. He saw a medium-sized man who seemed to be made of rawhide. His hair was black and curly, his skin dark. A bright scarf flashed color around his neck. Deep-set black eyes looked back at Gabe. The expression in them seemed guarded, perhaps even a little hostile . . . until Don Andres finished the introduction. "Jorge, this is Señor Conrad, the man I told you about."

Now Jorge's eyes lit up. "Ah . . . the man who grew up among the Indians. I am of Indian descent myself, Señor Conrad."

And obviously proud of it. Defiantly proud, Gabe guessed.

"Jorge," Don Andres said, "please show Señor Conrad to Dona Amelia's house." He turned toward Gabe, finally smiling. "If you like chili, señor, you will find plenty of it at that good lady's establishment. Chili that will teach your tongue good manners. But . . . if you will excuse me now, I have business to attend to."

The old man nodded and walked away toward the hotel dining room. Gabe, looking in through the dining room doors, could see Luis the waiter, hovering, anxiously awaiting the old man.

Gabe turned back toward Jorge. The *capataz* turned toward the front door. "If you will follow me, señor," he said politely.

"My name is Gabe," he replied. There was just a moment's hesitation on the other man's face, then he nodded and led the way out of the hotel.

Sonoratown was just a few blocks away. Here, the old adobes were ubiquitous. Large trees, obviously old, stood at street corners. Gabe liked the easy, open casualness of the place. "Why do they call it Sonoratown?" he asked.

Jorge snorted. "Because, since the Americanos came, since gold was discovered in the north, many Mexicans have come up from Sonora. Not always the best Mexicans, either—bandits, drunks, cheats. Greedy men. In the old days, we *Californios*, we who settled this land, not Californians, as the Yankees say, or *Californianos*, as the Mexicans call us, we who were born here, would not have tolerated these Mexicans. We would have sent them away with rope marks on their backs. Now, the Americanos, thinking that all of us with dark skin are from Sonora, call this place Sonoratown."

"And this Dona Amelia," Gabe asked, "is she also from Sonora?"

Jorge shook his head vigorously. "No, señor. She was born here, as was her father and his father before him. She is one of us."

This last statement was made with great pride. Gabe stole a quick look at the man walking beside him. A strong, open face. Gabe decided he liked him, liked the decisive way he moved, the apparent honesty of the man.

He liked him even better after they reached Dona Amelia's place. It was a long low adobe, tucked away behind another adobe. A widow, Dona Amelia had turned her home into a restaurant. The food was all that Don Andres had promised—tamales, fresh tortillas, meat, beans, everything covered with a wonderful chili sauce that soon had Gabe sweating.

As they ate, they talked. Jorge wanted to know about Gabe's people. "You do not look at all like an Indian," he said, obviously puzzled.

"My mother and father were both Americanos, from the East," Gabe explained. "They were on their way west, to California, when they were attacked by a band of the Bad Face Oglalas. The Oglala are a branch of the Lakota. What the White Men call the Sioux. My father was killed, my mother taken captive. She was pregnant at the time. I was born among the Oglala and raised as one of them until I was a young man."

He did not add that his father and mother had tried to enter the Black Hills, driven by gold fever. The Black Hills, sacred to the Lakota and Cheyenne. It had taken him years to forgive the father he'd never met for endangering his mother's life because of greed. His mother had later admitted to her own hunger for the yellow metal. He had not understood at first. It had taken him a while, living among the whites, before he could make sense of this hunger, this disease.

Neither did he tell Jorge that he had not left his people willingly.

The sound of Jorge's voice pulled him out of his reverie. "My grandfather, my mother's father, used to tell me about life among the Indians. He never accepted the fact that the Indian way of life was gone in California. The priests at the missions . . ."

"How about you?" Gabe asked abruptly. "Have you gotten used to it?"

Jorge's eyes widened a little in surprise. "Señor," he said, "I am a vaquero. I am a horseman. Half of my blood may be Indian, but the other half is *Californio*." Then his eyes grew bitter. "But that way of life is gone now, dying the way the Indian ways died. The Americanos. . . . if it were not for Don Andres . . ."

"An interesting man," Gabe said, gently probing. The old Spaniard fascinated him.

"The last of the Spanish rancheros," Jorge replied. "All the rest, wiped out, their ranches gone for taxes, debts, droughts. But not Don Andres. He still has his land, at least, part of it. *El Rancho de Las Palomas*. The Ranch of the Doves. And cattle. He still has cattle. And horses. Without horses, a man is less than a man, am I not right, señor?"

Gabe nodded. Who would agree with that more than someone brought up among the Oglala? Young Oglala boys were practically born on the back of a horse. Gabe himself had ridden since before he could walk.

Gabe reapplied himself to his meal, savoring the flavor of the corn meal in his tamale. "I'm surprised," he said, "the food being so good here at Dona Amelia's, that Don Andres is not eating with us."

Jorge's face showed a moment's shock. "But señor," he protested, "Don Andres is *Gente de Razon*. It would not be right for him to eat with his *capataz*. He is . . . well, he is . . . *El Patrón*!"

Gabe nodded. All the way across the Southwest, he'd noticed the class structure among the Latins. The old man was probably pure Spanish. A vast gulf divided him from those of mixed blood, or from anyone who worked with his hands. How disturbing the more classless Anglos must seem to him.

"You say that Don Andres is the last of the rancheros," Gabe prompted. "Why is that? I thought the old Spanish land grants were guaranteed after the Mexican war, in the Treaty of Guadalupe."

Jorge nearly spat. "Ah! The Treaty of Guadalupe. That badge of shame! That worthless scrap of paper!"

He relented a little. "Yes, señor, the old land grants were honored . . . if there were other pieces of paper available to satisfy the Yankee sense of law. If it was not too easy to lie and cheat. Many *Californios* kept their lands, those lands that were not stolen by the moneylenders. But then God seemed to turn his back on California, señor. Nature itself betrayed us—floods, droughts, grasshoppers, smallpox, and when there were no more cattle, the moneylenders attacked. They were the greatest plague of all. If Don Andres had not been clever, if the springs had not continued to flow at El Rancho de Las Palomas, if God had not been good to us, Don Andres would have lost his land, too. The land of his father and grandfather. Oh, we were hurt, señor, but we survived. And now Don Andres is building the ranch up again, the number of cattle are increasing, we have a fine horse herd. We can survive, señor. If . . ."

Jorge's face had turned cloudy. He looked down at his plate, loaded a fork with a tamale, but seemed undecided as to whether he really wanted to eat it. Gabe decided to pry.

"If?" he asked.

Jorge let the piece of tamale drop back onto his plate. He looked Gabe straight in the eye. "Money, señor. When there are Yankees near, money becomes very important. And there is danger in Yankee money. More danger than in anything that God or nature can throw at honest men. Terrible danger, señor. Danger that I think will finally destroy Don Andres and El Rancho de Las Palomas."

# CHAPTER THREE

Jorge returned his attention to his tamale, aimlessly pushing it around his plate. Gabe said nothing for a while, used a scrap of tortilla to sop up some of the fiery chili sauce. Finally, Gabe spoke. "Something's about to happen, isn't it?"

Jorge looked down at the battered remnants of his tamale. He seemed reluctant to answer. Finally, he nodded his head. "Yes. Don Andres has come to Los Angeles to borrow money, which he will use to buy machinery to take water from the spring and move it to where more cattle can get to it. We have all tried to talk him out of it, to tell him that only the Americanos have money now, and when they have money, they perform some kind of evil magic with it that takes away an honest man's cattle, his house, his land."

Interest, Gabe thought. Jorge must be talking about interest. He probably had little conception of its function . . . other than to hurt simple men. Interest. Usury. He wondered about Don Andres, wondered if the old man, lost in his world of vanished chivalry, had any conception of interest either. "How is Don Andres going to get this money?" he asked.

"There is a man who will lend it to him. Don Andres has already spoken to him. It sounds fair; we will fix the spring and pay the money back next year, when we sell some of the new calves. It is such a small amount, five hundred dollars."

"What about interest?"

Jorge shrugged. "I don't really understand this interest thing. The man says we will have to pay back about sixty dollars more than we borrowed. That seems like a lot, but Don Andres is determined to buy that equipment."

Gabe nodded doubtfully. The amount of interest seemed unusually small. He considered dismissing the subject, then decided to ask one more question. "Who is this man who is lending Don Andres the money?"

"A very friendly man. I met him earlier today. Don Andres said that his name is Sims."

Gabe, who had been vaguely thinking of ordering an enchilada, immediately looked up. "Is this Sims a fat man?" he demanded. "Does he wear a checkered suit? Does he talk a lot, as if he were nervous all the time?"

Jorge looked surprised. "Why . . . yes. That sounds like the man I met. Why? Do you know him?"

Gabe nodded grimly. "More or less."

Jorge studied the look on Gabe's face. "And you do not trust him."

Gabe remembered Sims's oily manner, his air of seedy desperation. If he was the man loaning Don Andres money, then the old man was in trouble. "No more than I'd trust a rattlesnake. We should warn Don Andres."

Jorge half-rose from his chair. "Yes. . . ."

Then he sat down again. "But how can we? If we interfere, if we question Don Andres's judgment, he will be offended. He will lose honor."

Damn, Gabe thought. Once again the old man was sounding like an Oglala war chief. Honor. Face. Better to be dead than to look bad. Maybe he should forget about the old man's troubles. Not interfere. If Don Andres was too stiff-necked to listen to advice, then let him sink.

But sink in a sea of Sims's making? He could not stand the thought of such a greasy specimen triumphing over the old man. He stood up abruptly. "There may be a way," he said.

"Señor?"

"There's a man here in Los Angeles that my grandfather told me to look up if I ever needed legal advice. He's a lawyer. According to my grandfather, he's one of the few honest ones. Which means something to me, because my grandfather is a lawyer, too, once again, one of the few honest ones. Let's go see this man."

After they'd paid and complimented Dona Amelia, Gabe and Jorge went out into the street. Since Los Angeles wasn't a very large town, it did not take them long to find the man they were looking for. Fifteen minutes after leaving the restaurant, they were standing in front of an office door on which were printed the words: "Major Horace Bell, Attorney at Law."

Gabe knocked. Footsteps approached the door from inside. The door opened. Gabe found himself facing a tall, handsome man with a huge, drooping, walrus moustache. "Major Bell?" Gabe asked.

The man spent a few seconds studying Gabe's appearance, then his eyes flicked to Jorge, who was standing a few paces to the rear. "Yes," he said. "I'm Bell. And who might you be?"

"Gabe Conrad. My grandfather told me you would be a good man to see if I needed legal help."

Bell was still studying Gabe carefully. Gabe was surprised by the suspicion in the other man's eyes. "My grandfather's name is Thomas Reid," Gabe added. "Of Boston."

Bell's eyes suddenly lit up. "Why didn't you say so right off? Thomas Reid! And you say you're his grandson?" Then Bell's eyes grew suspicious again. "Reid never told me he had a grandson."

Gabe decided not to tell Bell that his grandfather had not told anyone at all, because, until a few years ago, the old man hadn't had the slightest idea he even had a grandson. Bell didn't seem offended by his silence. Standing to one side, he invited the two of them in. Gabe and Jorge stepped into a small office. Bell offered them chairs, then sat opposite them, behind a large and battered desk.

Bell's suspicions still were evident in his expression. He spent five minutes questioning Gabe about his grandfather. Finally, he seemed satisfied that Gabe at least knew Thomas Reid. "And you do look a little like him," he admitted. "Especially the eyes. Pardon me for giving you such a hard time, but there are people here who would use any trick they could think of to cause me trouble."

Gabe said nothing, but his eyebrows raised a little. Bell responded to the silent question. "It's because of what's happened to this place over the last ten years. Especially the War. When war broke out, back in sixty-one, this town was full of Southern sympathizers. At least, that's what they called themselves, although damned few of them had the guts to go back to their beloved South and fight for it. Bayou trash. Thugs, mostly . . . bums, drunks, two-bit thieves, who'd been run out of the South. I went East, I fought for the Union, which is where I got that Major in front of my name. Fought damned hard, and when I came back to Los Angeles, they held my wartime service against me. California was more or less on its own during the War, and those so-called Southern sympathizers had pretty well taken over Los Angeles. They were just a mob, really, but there were so many of them that they were able to put their own kind into local offices: judges, sheriffs, prosecutors. Riffraff, all of them."

A wry smile passed across Bell's face. "Why, I remember the time a man was robbed up near Sepulveda Pass. He came into court to report it, but thought better of it when he saw that both the judge and the prosecutor were the men who'd robbed him. I've been fighting those bastards, and they've been fighting me, in their own cowardly way. Have to watch my back pretty carefully. I've taken a few of them down in the street, and I'll continue to do so until there are none left. Until this town is fit for decent folks again."

Bell suddenly looked sheepish. "Guess I've been running on. When I think about those scum, it gets my blood up. Now . . . what can I do for you?"

Gabe quickly recounted what Jorge had told him. "Oh, no," Bell said. "Not Andres Velasquez. I thought he had more sense."

"You think there's something wrong, then."

"Definitely. Especially since you mentioned Sims. Something fishy there. Sims couldn't come up with five hundred dollars to save his life. He must be fronting for someone else, some land-hungry bastard. You have to understand, one of the most common methods of prying loose those big land grants is through loan sharking. The old rancheros have no money sense at all. They're still living back in the sixteenth century. During the Spanish days, there never was much money in California, not in the form of cash. Just cattle and horses and land. Lots of land. Cash poor, every one of those old rancheros. Most of the things they needed they made by hand. And when the Yankee clippers started sailing around the Horn to California ports, the rancheros traded cattle hides for whatever they wanted to buy, things like laces for the ladies, tools, silver conchos and buckles to pretty up their horses. I was lucky. I got to see some of that trading. Came out here back in the early fifties. Just a tadpole, then."

Bell's eyes drifted off a little as he studied some fondly remembered inner scene. Then he shook himself. "Those old dons helped one another a lot . . . when they weren't fighting each other over politics. Loved a good party, dancing, singing, drinking, dueling. Whenever one of them needed anything, in a personal nature, there was usually a friend or acquaintance to do the giving. There was status in that, being generous. If a ranchero came to town and needed a few dollars to have a good time, he asked a friend for the money. Usually got it, too. And never thought of paying it back. A true *caballero* wouldn't insult his friend by paying him off like a loan shark. And how those old dons could spend! Which is where the loan sharks came in, after California became part of the Union. They'd loan a man maybe fifty dollars, at twelve and a half percent interest a *day*. Which meant nothing at all to the ranchero. He'd just sign this funny-looking piece of paper, written in a foreign language, and forget all about it. Had no conception of U. S. law. A year later, he'd discover that the interest, compounded daily, had boosted the loan up to maybe five thousand dollars. Of course, where was a cash poor land baron going to come up with five thousand dollars? So he'd sign a new note, extending the loan. And a few years later he'd owe more than the total value of all his land and cattle. He'd lose everything. And that's what I'm afraid is going to happen to Andres Velasquez. Why didn't he come and see me first?"

"Pride, I think," Gabe replied.

Bell nodded sourly. "That's what usually finishes them off. Can't accept advice."

"So you definitely think Don Andres is in trouble?"

"I certainly do. Maybe it's already too late. When did you say he was going to see this little thief, Sims?"

Gabe turned to Jorge and asked him in Spanish.

"In half an hour," the *capataz* replied. He hadn't been able to understand much of what Gabe and Bell had been talking about, but he'd been able to tell, from their tone, that it did not bode well for his *patrón*.

Bell thought for a moment. "We'll have to find a way to satisfy the old man's sense of honor. I think the best bet is simply to act as a lawyer." He turned to Jorge and asked him in Spanish if he was willing to take the heat if the whole thing backfired. Jorge nodded nervously.

Bell then questioned Jorge for several minutes, asking for any details he might have overheard about the loan. Finally, he sat down and began to write long lists of computations. "Let's see," he said. "From what you've told me, I suspect that the note will be for twelve and a half percent interest, compounded daily. That kind of interest is generally charged for much smaller loans. Somebody's out to ruin the old man, for sure. Now . . . twelve and a half percent a day against five hundred dollars . . ."

Bell filled several pages with hurriedly scribbled figures. "Got it," he finally said. He turned toward Jorge. "Now . . . where is Don Andres going to meet this little toad, Sims?"

"In his room at the hotel, señor."

Bell pulled out a big gold watch, glanced at it. "We'd better get moving, then. They meet in five minutes."

The three of them walked quickly over to the hotel. At the desk, Bell asked if anyone was with Don Andres. "Sure, Major," the desk clerk replied. "A Mr. Sims just went up to see him."

"No time to waste, then," Bell said, bounding up the stairs.

Once upstairs, Jorge led the way to Don Andres's room, then stood aside as Bell knocked. A moment later the door was opened by Don Andres himself. His eyes widened in surprise when he saw Bell, and behind him, Jorge and Gabe. "Yes?" he said, half in interrogation.

Looking past Don Andres, Gabe saw Sims seated at a table. A piece of paper lay on the tabletop in front of him. Sims was staring at Major Bell, obviously more than a little alarmed. Bell started to say something polite in Spanish, then looked past Don Andres, toward the table, the piece of paper, and Sims. "Ah," Bell said in fluent but accented Spanish, "I see that I have interrupted a business matter."

"You are never an interruption, Major," Don Andres said politely. Gabe could see that the old man liked Bell very much, but was impatient for him to leave.

"I should go, then, and come back later," Bell said. Gabe wondered what the hell he was trying to do. They should rush in now and stop this thing before it went too far, before Don Andres signed the note and accepted the five hundred dollars.

Bell was already turning as if to leave. Then he turned back to face Don Andres. "I wonder if you know about the new law," he said, almost offhandedly.

"Law?" Don Andres asked. "I know little of the law. Only that it usually brings trouble."

"Unfortunately, that is often the case," Bell replied. "Still . . . what can an honest man do, but try to live within the law?"

Don Andres was looking just a little bit confused. "This new law," he finally asked, "what is it about?"

Bell shrugged apologetically. "It says that whenever a piece of legal paper is signed, in any type of business negotiation, that an officer of the court must be present. Such as a judge or a lawyer."

Gabe, impressed by Bell's audacity and inventiveness, watched as Don Andres studied the lawyer's face for a moment. "Ah," the old man finally said. "Then perhaps you had better come inside."

But now Sims, who clearly understood only part of what Major Bell and Don Andres were saying to one another, half-rose from his chair. "I don't know what the hell you think you're doing here, Bell," he blurted in English, "but I protest your presence. This is a private business transaction."

Bell was already walking toward the table and the piece of paper sitting on top of it. Gabe moved around Bell and headed toward Sims, who had, until now, aimed most of his attention at the lawyer. Sims's eyes widened a little when he recognized Gabe.

Gabe stopped a few feet away, his weight on the balls of his feet. "Perhaps you'd like to do your protesting to me," he said coldly, in English. "Outside, in the hall. I'd hate to see blood all over this beautiful carpet."

For just a moment, Sims glared defiance. Then he was caught by Gabe's eyes, by their cold intensity, all of it directed straight at him. "I . . ." he muttered, "I just . . ."

Bell walked straight to the table and picked up the note. "A loan, I see," he said to Don Andres. "The note is very well written. Quite legal."

Don Andres nodded, apparently reassured. Bell continued speaking. "I see that it is for five hundred dollars, due in a year."

Don Andres nodded.

"Interesting, this clause," Bell said, pointing to a paragraph. Don Andres nodded with a little less certainty; the note was in English, and he did not read English. "Yes," Bell said. "Twelve and a half percent interest, compounded daily."

Don Andres nodded. "Señor Sims has explained the matter of the interest to me."

"Hmm," Bell murmured. "A bit high." He glanced up from the note, looking Don Andres straight in the face. "You understand, then, how much you will have to pay back at the end of a year? As an officer of the court, I must ask you this."

"Of course," Don Andres replied, a little stiffly. "Señor Sims has explained it all. . . ."

"Fifty thousand dollars. Due in one year," Bell said softly.

For a moment the words did not seem to register with Don Andres. He glanced away, toward the window, distractedly. Then he turned back toward Bell, his movements suddenly stiff, awkward. "*Cincuenta mil dólares?*" he asked, his voice full of wonder.

Bell nodded, looking the old man straight in the face. Don Andres remained standing stiffly for another few seconds, then he turned, looking toward the bed. Gabe saw that an ornate gun belt had been looped over one of the bedposts. The pearl-handled butt of a revolver protruded from the holster. Don Andres turned back to look at Sims. His face was beginning to darken. His eyes were cold, hooded. He turned around again and started walking toward the gun belt. Sims began to look alarmed.

"Hey!" he blurted. "What the hell is going on here?"

Gabe smiled. "I think Don Andres is going to kill you," he replied.

Sims jerked erect from his chair. "Oh . . . God no," he murmured. "They said the old man wouldn't . . ."

Don Andres was still heading for the gun belt. Jorge moved to stand in his way. "*Patrón . . .*" he murmured.

Don Andres's head twisted toward his *capataz*. Anger tugged at his features. "Jorge . . . damn your insolence," he said icily. "Get out of my way."

Bell looked at Sims, pointed toward the door. "If you want to keep on living . . ." he said.

In four hurried strides, Sims was out the door. Everyone in the room could hear his boots pounding hurriedly down the stairs. Don Andres was still glaring at Jorge. Bell looked at Gabe, then at the door. Gabe nodded. Time to leave. Don Andres caught the interplay between Gabe and Bell out of the corner of his eye. He tore his gaze away from Jorge, turned to face the two men. His words, as well as his face, were stiff when he finally spoke. "Señores," he said. "I owe you both a great debt. However, I would like to be alone now . . . with Jorge."

Major Bell gave a little bow. "Of course, Don Andres." He started toward the door, with Gabe a couple of steps ahead of him, but turned just before stepping through the doorway. "I have a friend who loans money," he said to the old man. "He is honest. If you would like to borrow five hundred dollars from him, in six months you will be expected to pay back only six hundred dollars."

Before the old man could answer, Bell was in the hallway, following Gabe toward the stairs. Don Andres watched the two men go, then slowly shut the door. He stood leaning against it for a moment, then turned to face his foreman. "Jorge Gonzalez," he said in a cold, cutting voice. "You have interfered in my business. You have encouraged outsiders to intrude upon by private affairs. What do you have to say for yourself?"

For a few seconds, Jorge felt dread sweep over him as he stared into his master's cold, hard face. Then, surprising both himself and Don Andres, he stood erect and answered boldly. "I could not stand by and watch Yankee thieves steal El Rancho de Las Palomas. You must not forget, *Patrón*, that I was born there. It is my home as well as yours."

Amazement washed the anger from the old man's face. For several seconds he was unable to say anything at all. When he finally spoke, his tone was much more humble, as humble as possible for a man of his background. "Forgive me, my friend," he said softly. "I have been a fool, and you have saved me from my foolishness."

Jorge suddenly felt abashed. "*Patrón*," he murmured, staring down at the intricate pattern on the carpet, "if I have offended, if I have been presumptuous . . ."

"Nonsense," Don Andres replied sharply, all the normal arrogance back in his voice. "It is over. We will talk of this no more."

Jorge nodded silently.

"Except for one last thing," Don Andres continued. "I order that once a month you remind me how fortunate I am to have with me a man as courageous and loyal as yourself."

Jorge nodded again. Both men knew this would never happen, that neither would ever again speak of what had just taken place. But Jorge felt a glow of gratitude sweep over him that the words had even been spoken. "Of course, *Patrón*," he murmured. Then he headed for the door. There was one last nod between the two men, and then the matter was indeed closed. The terrible weight of Castilian pride had been adequately satisfied.

# CHAPTER FOUR

After Gabe and Major Bell left the Pico House, they stood together for a moment beneath the hotel's arcade. "Thanks for your help," Gabe said to the major.

Bell smiled, stuck out his hand. "All in a day's work. You know how I feel about scum like Sims. But what about you? What made you go out of your way to help someone whom I suspect you don't even know very well?"

Gabe took Bell's hand, shook it briefly, and shrugged. "Maybe I feel the same way about men like Sims."

Bell nodded. "Yes. But I still think Sims was fronting for someone else. I don't believe this is going to stop here. Someone's after Don Andres's land. Now that the loan thing didn't work, they'll try some other way."

Gabe nodded. "I suspect you're right. What do you think will happen next?"

Just as Bell shrugged, Gabe caught sight of furtive movement further down the street. Without turning his head, he glanced in that direction. It was Sims, slipping along the boardwalk, glancing back worriedly in their direction. Gabe saw Sims dart in through the door of one of the town's fancier saloons. Gabe realized that Major Bell had not spotted Sims. "Thanks again, Major," Gabe said. Bell touched his hat in farewell, and the two men turned away from one another.

Gabe started toward the saloon. Then he stopped himself. He knew Sims was up to something, knew it from the furtive way he'd been moving. He'd like to know what that something was, but if he barged straight in the front door, Sims would see him, would become even more evasive.

Most likely the saloon had a back door. Gabe walked around the block. An alley cut off from the main street, running behind the saloon. Gabe walked down the alley and knew he reached the saloon when he saw a pile of boxes filled with empty bottles. There was a door next to the boxes. It opened easily. Gabe stepped inside. A short hallway lay ahead. Doors branched off to the sides, apparently storerooms. Another door lay at the end of the hallway. Gabe eased it open a crack. Peering through the narrow opening, Gabe was able to look straight into the saloon's main room. Not more than twenty feet away, Sims was sitting at a table, across from a well-dressed man. The man looked angry.

"Damn it, Sims," Gabe heard the man snarl, "you could foul up eating breakfast."

"But Mr. Barnes," Sims whined, "it was going fine until Major Bell and that man with the long hair barged in. I can't understand how they knew. . . ."

The man whom Sims had called Barnes snorted derisively. "You've already told me that the old man's foreman was with them. He must have known about the loan and told the others. But how Bell got involved in the whole thing . . . That damned Bell will have to go someday. Coddles these damned greasers."

"Well, I tried, Mr. Barnes. Tried real hard. And you said . . . about the hundred dollars . . ."

"Trying isn't good enough," Barnes snapped. "I ought to . . . Oh hell, here's twenty dollars. And I don't want to see your whining face anywhere around me again. Do you understand?"

Barnes slapped a twenty dollar gold piece down onto the table. Sims seemed disappointed for a moment that it was not the hundred he had hoped for, but he scooped up the gold piece anyhow. With the money in his hand, he twisted around in his seat and turned toward the bar, as if about to call out to the bartender for a drink, but Barnes grabbed Sims by the sleeve and jerked him around so that they were face-to-face. "You aren't drinking in here with me, you little creep," Barnes snarled. "Get the hell out of here. I have to think."

Sims's face darkened with anger, but true to form, he did not have the courage to protest. He got jerkily to his feet, backed away from the table, then started toward the saloon's front door. He was halfway to the door when he performed one small act of defiance. Stopping at the bar, he talked with the bartender for a moment. Gabe watched the bartender sell Sims a bottle of whiskey. Now that he was far enough away from Barnes to have grown a little courage, Sims glared back at Barnes, bottle in hand. Then he walked out the door. Gabe noticed that Barnes was not even looking in Sims's direction. but sat motionless, obviously deep in thought, staring down at the tabletop.

Gabe softly shut the door and walked back down the hallway and out into the alley. He debated following Sims, getting him alone, pumping him for information about Barnes, but he decided that was not necessary. It was obvious that Barnes was the one who'd put Sims up to offering Don Andres the loan. And for an obvious purpose—to take the old man's land. No, Sims was a dead end, a tool used once and now discarded. Barnes himself was the one to watch.

When Gabe reached the main street, he saw Jorge leaving the Pico House. He walked straight up to him. Jorge saw him coming. "I want to thank you," Jorge started to say. "If it had not been for your help . . ."

Gabe read the embarrassment on the foreman's face. "Forget it," he said. "There are other problems. Do you know anything about a man named Barnes?"

Jorge's face showed surprise. "Barnes? A smooth-looking man with a cold face? Very well-dressed?"

Gabe nodded. "He was talking to Sims. He was very angry that the loan didn't go through. He was the one who put Sims up to it."

"Ah, yes," Jorge said. "That makes sense. This Mr. Barnes has been trying to get Don Andres to sell the ranch. For a ridiculously small price. Don Andres, of course, has refused."

Gabe nodded. "The loan, then, was his way of forcing the issue. But I know he's not going to stop there. We ought to tell Don Andres."

Jorge spread his hands helplessly. "Señor, I think it would not be wise to say anything more of this matter for a day or two. At the moment Don Andres is feeling like an old grizzly bear with a thorn in its paw."

Gabe nodded. Don Andres's Castilian pride again. But, what could be done . . . except gather more information? He said good-bye to Jorge, then headed once again for Major Bell's office.

The major was surprised to see him. "Something wrong?" he asked. "I sent my friend over to the hotel to lend Don Andres the money. Don't tell me there's more trouble."

Gabe sat down across from Bell's desk. "Do you know a man named Barnes?"

Bell looked surprised. "Henry Barnes?" Then comprehension swept over his face. "Now I guess you're going to tell me that he's the one who was behind Sims."

Gabe quickly told Bell about the conversation he'd overheard. Bell shook his head sadly. "That's bad news. Henry Barnes is a ruthless man. If he's after Don Andres's land, he'll keep after it until he has it."

"But why? Why particularly Don Andres's land?"

Bell shrugged. "Why not? It's good land, and there's been talk of a railroad being built out that way. Not that I believe it." His eyes flashed angrily. "That damned railroad is going to go through Los Angeles! It has to!"

He shook his head. "Either way, for the past couple of years Barnes has been building up big land holdings down here in the southern part of the state, the same way John Irvine has done in the next county down. Irvine has wheeled and dealed and stolen, and he has more damned land than he knows what to do with. Barnes wants to follow in his footsteps, but I suspect that Barnes is even more ruthless than Irvine. He wants to sew up as much land as possible. Hell, everyone knows it's only a matter of time until the railroad comes through here. Then southern California is going to boom. It's got the climate, the natural resources, the only thing it lacks is people. And when the railroad finally gets here, the people will come flooding in. You mark my words, Los Angeles is going to be a metropolis some day. It'll pass San Francisco; there's no room to expand up there."

Gabe said nothing as he watched a flush of excitement redden Bell's face. So this man, too, was another white man who saw good only in growth and expansion. Perhaps the main difference between Bell and men like Barnes was that Bell was not willing to steal, lie, and cheat to realize this growth.

There was not much more to say. Bell saw Gabe to the door. "You'd better warn Don Andres," he said. "Henry Barnes is a dangerous man."

"Of course," Gabe promised. But he knew that warning the old man would only make him stubborn. He'd have to keep an eye on Barnes himself and hope Don Andres got out of town once he had his money.

Walking back to the hotel, he wondered why he was involving himself so deeply in someone else's trouble. Why not just leave Los Angeles and ride to where he wanted to go . . . the ocean? Then he had an image of the old man's proud, hawk-like face, and as he held that image, it slowly faded into the image of Red Cloud, the war chief with whom he'd ridden against the soldiers, in that sometimes victorious, but ultimately hopeless struggle to save the People's way of life from the encroachment of the White Man.

Was Don Andres's struggle equally as hopeless? Probably. But Gabe would be damned if he'd simply ride away and leave the old man to fight alone. He had to do something. He headed back toward the saloon. Maybe Barnes was still there, maybe not.

He was. As Gabe walked in through the door, the front one this time, he saw Barnes sitting at the same table as before, but this time, there were four men with him. Hard-looking men.

Gabe had had the foresight to tuck his hair up underneath his hat. He doubted Barnes knew him by sight, probably only had Sims's description of his long hair. The deception seemed to be working; Barnes barely looked in his direction.

Gabe sat at a table. The bartender, sighing, came around the end of the bar and walked over. "What'll it be, mister?"

Gabe almost asked for his usual, sarsaparilla or root beer. He hated alcohol, hated what it had done to his people, but he stopped himself. Ordering sarsaparilla in a bar excited comment, and he definitely did not want to attract attention. He ordered a beer, with no intention of drinking it.

While the bartender was drawing his beer, Gabe covertly watched Barnes's table. Both Barnes and the four men were leaning inward, with their heads close together. Barnes was talking earnestly. Gabe saw him slip a small leather bag across the table to one of the men. The bag looked heavy, and when the man picked it up, Gabe heard it clink. Gold. Probably quite a bit of gold. And, looking at the four men, at their hard faces, and the guns that hung at their sides, he had little doubt as to what the money was for.

The bartender brought Gabe's beer. Gabe paid him, mimed a sip of the beer, then got up and left the saloon. It took him fifteen minutes, wandering through Sonoratown, to find Jorge. The *capataz* was in a small cantina, sipping tequila. He looked up, surprised, when Gabe walked in. One look at Gabe's face was enough. "More trouble?" Jorge asked.

Gabe told him about Barnes and the four hardcases. "Gunmen, for sure," Gabe said grimly. "I'm sure Barnes has paid them to kill Don Andres. We have to get him out of town."

Jorge laughed bitterly. "Don Andres will go when he wants to go and not before. He's so hardheaded, that old man, that sometimes I . . . Ah . . . *mierda*!"

Nevertheless, Gabe talked Jorge into making preparations. Both men went to the Pico House stables together.

Gabe saddled his horse, while Jorge readied both his and Don Andres's mounts. Then Gabe went into the hotel and collected his gear. After checking out, he went back to the stables and lashed his gear onto his horse. Jorge came in a few minutes later, loaded down with his and Don Andres's belongings.

"I had to sneak into the *patrón's* room like a thief," Jorge complained as he lashed the gear into place. "While Don Andres was downstairs in the bar. I don't know how I'll ever get him outside."

"Do your best," Gabe said tersely. "Meanwhile, I'll look around."

They talked together for a few more minutes, then Gabe nodded good-bye to Jorge and mounted his horse. He rode out into the street, around to the front of the hotel, where he tied the horse to a hitching post. Dismounting, he slipped his Winchester from its saddle scabbard, then walked across the street. It was a measure of Los Angeles's rawness that he was able to walk along the town's main street, carrying a rifle, without arousing undue interest. He settled himself onto a veranda, in front of a general store directly across from the Pico House, where he could watch the entrance. Nothing to do now but wait.

A few minutes later he saw Jorge pass by, leading his and Don Andres's horses, fully outfitted for travel. Jorge tied the animals to a hitching rack in front of the hotel's main entrance, close to Gabe's horse. Then he went inside. Another ten minutes passed. Jorge had explained to Gabe that he was going to tell the old man that he'd overheard a plot to rob him of the five hundred dollars he'd just borrowed, the money needed to improve the spring. He'd told Gabe that he'd never get the old man to leave town on grounds of personal safety, but if it was something that affected the welfare of El Rancho de Las Palomas, well, that was a different matter entirely.

Gabe stiffened. The four hardcases who'd been talking to Barnes had just come into view, walking toward the Pico House. Damn! If they'd only held off a few more minutes.

Because he also caught sight of Jorge and Don Andres, walking out the hotel's main entrance.

The gunmen were to Gabe's left. He watched them fan out in the middle of the street. Don Andres and Jorge were to Gabe's right, walking toward their horses, which were across the street from him. Jorge noticed the gunmen before Don Andres did. He tried to steer the old man toward the horses, but one of the gunmen called out, "Hey! Greaser! You with the funny hat!"

Gabe doubted that Don Andres could understand more than a few of the words the man used. But he could understand the tone. His head came around, and he studied the man and his companions intently. Jorge was pulling at his arm, trying to get him closer to the horses, but the old man angrily shook off Jorge's hand, then took a step toward the four men in the middle of the street.

Gabe saw that Don Andres was wearing the fancy gun belt he'd seen before in the old man's room. The butt of a pearl-handled Colt revolver thrust out of the gun belt's holster. Gabe saw Don Andres's hand move closer to the pistol. "Do I hear dogs barking?" the old man said scornfully, his voice sharp and cutting.

Gabe felt a burst of admiration for Don Andres. Two to four odds, and against heavily armed men. Each of the gunmen had two revolvers, and all carried big knives in sheaths at their sides. Very bad odds. Almost suicidal odds. Then it occurred to Gabe that perhaps the old man did not care if he died, as long as it was in a hard fight. The culture he'd grown up in had been destroyed around him by the dregs of gringo society—thieves and businessmen, as if there were a difference between the two. Men who stole by lending money. Perhaps Don Andres believed that in the end he too would lose his ranch, no matter what he did, lose the land on which his ancestors were buried. Perhaps he simply did not wish to live long enough to see that happen.

Gabe was already stepping into the street, his rifle held by his side, the muzzle pointed in the general direction of the four gunmen. The head of the man who'd insulted Don Andres swiveled toward Gabe. Gabe noticed that the man had cold eyes. The eyes of a killer. "Butt out, mister," the man snapped. "This don't concern you."

"I think it does," Gabe replied flatly. "Make your move or back off."

Gabe stepped further to his right, until he was about fifteen feet from Jorge and Don Andres. Gabe did not like the way the two *Californios* were standing, too close together, so that all four of the gunmen could concentrate on them. With Gabe to the side, the gunmen would have to split their concentration.

"Señor," Gabe heard Don Andres call out to him, "this is not your fight."

"I'm making it my fight," Gabe retorted, never taking his eyes from the two gunmen closest to him.

He did not know how it started, perhaps Don Andres drew first, but one of the gunmen farthest from him reached for his pistol. Triggered by this first movement, all seven men exploded into action. Loud gunfire rang out. Gabe, with his rifle already in his hand, fired the first shot, putting a bullet into the stomach of the man closest to him. By the time Gabe levered another round into the chamber, the next gunman already had his pistol in his hand. He fired, too hurriedly, the bullet whistling past Gabe's head. Shooting from the hip, Gabe shot him twice through the body.

He turned toward Don Andres and Jorge. He was surprised to see that the two remaining gunmen were down; apparently Don Andres and Jorge could shoot. But one of the gunmen was half-sitting, with his left hand pressed against a patch of blood low down on his side. He still held his pistol in his other hand. As Don Andres fired again, missing this time, the man raised his pistol and fired back. Gabe saw Don Andres stagger and almost drop his weapon.

Then Gabe's rifle and the pistols of both Jorge and Don Andres opened up again, and the man was knocked over backward by the weight of lead slamming into his body.

Gabe quickly tracked his rifle barrel over the four downed gunmen. None of them were moving. Now that the action was over, he realized it could not have lasted more than ten or fifteen seconds, a prolonged blast of gunfire that had ended four lives and wounded another man.

All other activity in the street had come to a halt with the first shot, but now that the killing was over, Gabe saw cautious heads poke out from behind wagons, barrels, and doorways. "What the hell?" someone called out haltingly.

Carefully, still carrying his rifle at the ready, Gabe walked over to Don Andres and Jorge. Jorge was supporting the old man, who had a large patch of blood on the left side of his vest. "How bad is he hit?" Gabe asked Jorge.

"I don't know," Jorge replied.

Don Andres tried to push Jorge away. "It's nothing," he said, his voice tight with pain. "I do not need help."

But he staggered when he tried to stand on his own. "Get him on his horse," Gabe snapped to Jorge. "Get him the hell out of here."

"I will not run away," Don Andres protested. "It was a fair fight. . . ."

"Shut up!" Gabe snapped, startling the old man. "You're not the only one involved here. Can't you, for just once in your arrogant life, think of anything but your damned pride?"

Don Andres stood, openmouthed. Gabe wondered if anyone had ever talked to the old man that way. And lived. But he had other worries. People were beginning to gather. People he'd rather not see. People such as Henry Barnes, who had come out of the saloon where Gabe had last seen him and was walking along the boardwalk in their direction.

Barnes had probably been watching the whole fight, and what he had seen had obviously not pleased him. It had not been intended to come out this way. Gabe saw a flush of anger on Barnes's face. The gold he'd given the hardcases was gone, and the man he wanted dead was still on his feet. But he was a fast thinker, Gabe had to hand him that. Someone else had blurted out the obvious question, "What the hell happened?" and Barnes jumped right on it.

"I saw the whole thing," he shouted. "The two Mexes and that long-haired bastard shot down those boys in cold blood. Just opened up on 'em from behind, cut 'em down."

Other voices rose in protest, those who'd actually seen it happen, or at least part of it, but those moderate, quieter voices were drowned out by louder, angrier cries from the growing crowd. "Get the sheriff!" someone shouted.

"Hell, we don't need no damned sheriff," someone else shouted back. "We kin handle this ourselves."

Gabe looked at the faces around him, more and more people were gathering, mostly men, mostly the kind of faces Major Bell had warned him about. This was the famous Los Angeles mob, two-bit grifters, highwaymen, Southern sympathizers, drunks, bums. Los Angeles was well-known for the propensity of its seamier citizens to lynch first, ask questions later. Anything to brighten up a dull day.

But the mob was not accustomed to facing a determined man with a loaded rifle. Gabe saw that Jorge had hoisted Don Andres up onto his horse, a big white animal with fancy horse furniture. Don Andres slumped in the saddle, but he had the reins firmly in his left hand. Gabe saw the old man reach down with his right and fill his hand with the pearl-handled pistol. Jorge had his pistol out, too.

Gabe moved sideways to his horse and mounted. From the saddle, he was able to overlook the crowd. He jerked his head toward the dead gunmen. "Those hardcases were hired to kill the old man," he called out. He pointed toward Barnes. "By that man. They didn't do a very good job. Now . . . we're riding out of here. Anyone who tries to stop us can join those four clowns. Dead."

Gabe pulled his horse around, but kept the muzzle of his rifle tracking over the crowd. Several men flinched away, as much from the light in Gabe's eyes as from the threat of the rifle. Gabe saw that Jorge and Don Andres had already started to ride away down the street. He rode along after them, still keeping an eye on the crowd. He passed close to Barnes, who was still up on the boardwalk. He pinned Barnes with his gaze. "I ought to kill you now, Barnes," Gabe said coldly. For the first time, he saw Barnes lose color and turn pale, but the man still stood his ground.

Gabe had to fight back the urge to put a bullet through Barnes's head. It always made sense to kill your enemy when you had the chance; he'd failed to do it once before, and it had cost him. And had cost others. But he knew that if he gunned down Barnes in cold blood, in front of a couple of dozen witnesses, he'd hang for sure. "Another time," he said softly to Barnes. Then he rode off down the street, after Jorge and Don Andres.

# CHAPTER FIVE

They rode south for an hour. At first, Don Andres sat fairly straight in the saddle, then he began to slump toward his wounded side. Gabe called a halt. He and Jorge helped Don Andres dismount, then they cut away part of his shirt to look at the wound.

Gabe decided it could have been worse; the bullet had gone through the muscles just below the ribs. A clean wound, the bullet was gone. He doubted it had passed through deep enough to damage the intestines or stomach. But Don Andres had lost blood; he was weakening. Gabe bound up the wound as best he could, and they remounted, but within a few miles he saw that sitting a horse, with Don Andres's muscles flexing in time to the animal's gait, was causing more blood to leak from the wound.

Gabe turned to Jorge and said quietly, "We have to find some other way for him to travel. He's going to bleed to death in the saddle."

Jorge nodded. "I have been thinking the same. Only a little way ahead there is the house of a friend. They will help us."

Sure enough, just the other side of a ridge they came upon a collection of adobes, a combination ranch and farm. Apparently, from the number of children who gathered to see them ride into the yard, this was the home of several families.

As they approached the door of the largest adobe, a middle-aged man came out to meet them. He smiled up at Don Andres . . . until he noticed the bloodstained bandage wrapped around his lower torso. Turning, he shouted orders into the house. A moment later three women came running, and from the surrounding adobes, other men appeared.

Don Andres, still stubborn, showing no evidence of the pain he had to be feeling, started to dismount by himself. Jorge and Gabe had to catch him to keep him from falling. White-faced but forcing a smile, Don Andres turned to face the middle-aged man. "Juan . . . my pardon for disturbing your afternoon."

The old man was hustled into the house, where he was guided to a bed. The oldest of the three women, (Gabe could not tell whether she was in her forties or her sixties) supervised as Don Andres's wound was cleaned, then bandaged neatly. Food was called for. Gabe and Jorge ate ravenously; Don Andres, lying down, picked at his food. Gabe looked at the old Spaniard closely. His face was grey with pain and fatigue. Juan noticed the same thing. "He must rest for several days," he insisted.

Gabe shook his head. "I don't know if that will be possible. There was . . . trouble in Los Angeles. Four men are dead, and there are people there who would like to cause Don Andres more trouble. We may have to move on, in case they follow."

Juan's mouth formed into stubborn lines. "Let them try to get at him here. We will—"

"No, my old friend," Don Andres said from the bed. "I will not bring trouble down on your house."

"Ridiculous!" Juan snapped back. "Since when has helping a friend been considered trouble?"

Jorge shook his head. "We are grateful for the offer, Juan, but there are people who will stop at nothing to kill Don Andres. If we stay here, and they discover where we are, as they eventually must, they will merely wait until we are ready to leave, and all that time they will be gathering more strength. No, we must take Don

Andres back to El Rancho de Las Palomas. There, he will be safe."

Now Gabe cut in. "Might be a good idea, though, to check our back trail."

Juan nodded, seeing the logic. "Yes. I will gather some men. Meanwhile, we can start Don Andres south, in a wagon."

Within twenty minutes, men were riding in from the general area, all of Spanish decent, a wild-looking bunch. They impressed Gabe; they were obviously delighted by the idea of a good fight. While Juan organized the men, fifteen of them, Don Andres was helped out of the house and into a wagon. The riders waited until the old man was on his way out of the ranch yard, guarded by another half dozen men, then they galloped away from the adobes, yelping wildly. Gabe rode with them, yelping just as loudly. He had not felt so good since the last time he'd ridden out with an Oglala war party.

They'd traveled less than a mile when they saw a small group of riders approaching, a dozen of them. The men with Gabe fanned out, stationing themselves at points that dominated the trail.

As the other riders drew closer, Gabe saw that Barnes was one of them. The rest were ragtag members of the usual Los Angeles mob. They drew up about forty yards from the Spaniards. Barnes immediately recognized Gabe. Barnes turned to a man next to him and said something in a low voice. Gabe could not hear the words. The man Barnes was speaking to was one of the few really dangerous-looking men in the group.

Barnes swept his eyes over the Spaniards. "Get out of our way. We're after some killers." He pointed to Gabe. "And that man's one of 'em."

There was no response from the Spaniards, except the simultaneous cocking of fifteen rifles. Gabe saw most of the men with Barnes turn pale, except for the hard-looking man next to him.

"Hey," one of the Los Angeles riders muttered, "I didn't know there was gonna be so many of 'em."

Gabe rode forward, his Winchester in his right hand, cocked, the muzzle pointed high, but ready to swing down toward Barnes. "When we left Los Angeles," he said to Barnes, "after your hired gunhands tried to murder Don Andres, I told you that I'd kill you later. Maybe now's the time."

Gabe watched as rage, hatred, and fear warred on Barnes's face. "No, mister," Barnes finally said, his voice tight. "Now isn't the time. But you're going to regret the day you got involved in this."

Barnes turned in the saddle. "Come on, boys," he called out to the men around him. "Let's get on back to town."

No one protested; most of the Los Angeles men seemed relieved that there wasn't going to be a fight. At least, not a fight in which the odds were not completely in their favor. Gabe watched in contempt as Barnes and his men turned their horses and rode quickly away, back toward Los Angeles. He would have welcomed a fight, welcomed a chance to get rid of Barnes for good. The man was trouble. He was certain he would see him again, and maybe the next time the odds would be heavily in Barnes's favor.

Juan sat his horse for a few minutes, until the Los Angeles men had disappeared over a hill. "We'll ride after them for a while," he said to Gabe. "In case they try to circle around us."

Gabe nodded. "Fine. I'll head back to Don Andres. I'm sure he's grateful for all you have done."

Juan smiled, a beautiful flash of teeth. "My pleasure, señor. If I told you all the things Andres Velasquez has done for me, we would be talking all day."

Gabe turned his horse and rode back down the trail. He turned, once, and saw Juan and his men disappearing over the hill where they'd last seen Barnes. That should keep the Los Angeles men at bay for a while. Now, he and Jorge had to get the old man home, where he could heal.

Within half an hour, Gabe saw the wagon and its outriders ahead of him. He could not see Don Andres. When he reached the wagon, he realized that the old man was lying down in the wagon bed, on a straw mattress. He seemed to be sleeping. Gabe noticed that his color was better.

Jorge rode over to Gabe. "No trouble?" he asked.

Gabe shrugged. "Barnes showed up with a mob. They didn't have the stomach for a fight. Juan and his men are making sure they don't come after us. How long before we reach the ranch?"

Jorge looked sourly at the slow-moving wagon. "At this speed, two or three days. It's a long way, señor. El Rancho de Las Palomas is a very isolated ranch, which is why we have been left alone so long. But now, with the Yankees buying up all the land, we are suddenly desirable."

"Yes. I know how that is," Gabe said curtly, remembering how, once the White Man had begun to covet various Indian lands, the old way of life had been destroyed forever.

By nightfall they had reached the small settlement of Santa Ana. Jorge guided them to another complex of adobes, the home of more friends of Don Andres. They spent the night securely, with rotations of guards watching for intruders. By the time they were ready to resume their journey the next morning, Gabe was pleased to see that Don Andres looked much better, although from the ginger-ly way he moved, his wound had stiffened considerably.

After a hearty breakfast, replete with chili and tortillas, they set out again, Don Andres still in the wagon, lying down. South of Santa Ana they passed through a long, lovely valley, with smooth rolling hills on either side. The land was very dry. Gabe commented on the sere brown vegetation.

"Of course," Jorge replied. "This is the end of the dry season. It has hardly rained at all for the past six or seven months. Fortunately, the rains should start any day."

"You mean it actually rains in California?" Gabe said.

Jorge laughed. "You'll find out. But of course, this is a very dry land, the rains only come for a small part of the year, sometimes in disastrous amounts, too quickly, and then we have floods. But, in general, water is scarce in this entire southern area. Only if you have a good spring or a deep well, do you have a chance of survival. And even then . . ." Jorge sighed.

"You make is sound like a very hard land." Gabe smiled sympathetically.

"Oh, yes, it can be hard. It can also be lovely, soft, like living in a waking dream. But lack of water . . . and in the past, the Indians . . ."

"Yes," Gabe replied, with just a touch of bitterness. "I suppose they wanted their land back."

Jorge recognized the other man's bitter tone. "It wasn't quite like that here. There were never very many Spaniards in California, possibly five or six thousand in this entire huge country, from San Diego all the way up to Sonoma. Hundreds of miles of mostly empty land. In the whole of what is now San Diego County, there were never more than six hundred of us. Most of the Indians who came into contact with the Spanish lived on the mission lands. Not always willingly, of course, but to their descendants, those born at the missions, it was home. Their land. And then, about forty years ago, when California became part of Mexico, the Mexican government broke up the missions, took them away from the Church, and decreed that the land was to go to the people who had worked it, made it rich. It was to go to the Indian laborers."

Jorge shrugged. "But you know how it is. When there's wealth to be divided, it seldom goes to those who deserve it. A few Spaniards gobbled up all that rich mission land, and some of it was very, very rich. There were missions with tens of thousands of cattle, thousands of horses, hundreds of acres under cultivation. And when the powerful men, the *Gente de Razon* took this land, they pushed the Indians out, or made laborers of them, made them poor again. On their own land, the land the government meant them to have. But Mexico City is far away . . ."

Gabe said nothing. He was fascinated by one of the terms Jorge had used. *Gente de Razon*, the people who ran California in Spanish days, the words meaning "people with the power of reason, of thought." At least, as they understood reasoning. A class system, with the Indians at the bottom, men like Jorge, half-Indian, in the middle, and the Don Andreses on top. Except they were not on top anymore. The Yankees were, and the old Spanish dons were having trouble accepting it.

He glanced over at the wagon. Don Andres had fallen asleep again. To talk of class systems and their injustice would mean nothing to the old man. To him, it was simply the way God had ordered the world. Gabe began to realize that it was not for Don Andres that he was involving himself in the struggle against Barnes. It was for men like Jorge.

Jorge was still reminiscing. "Many of the mission Indians were angry at the way they'd been cheated. They left the missions, which were now ranchos, and went inland, to join their wild Indian cousins. They made war on us. At one time most of the Spanish people in what is now San Diego County had to move into the pueblo at San Diego, or be killed. But not Don Andres. He had always treated the Indians well. Even that might not have protected him, but some years before, he had saved the life of an Indian chief, a man from one of the most warlike tribes, and this man saw to it that he was not molested. At least, not more than we could handle."

Gabe nodded. Without a doubt, Don Andres was a just man, at least, within his understanding of justice. "Yet," he said, "times must be hard, if Don Andres had to go all the way to Los Angeles to borrow five hundred dollars. Perhaps the Yankees have made it impossible for you to survive."

Jorge laughed, with just a trace of irony. "Oh, not at first. When the Yankees took over, many *Californios* were pleased. Not me, not Don Andres, but some. They even helped the Yankees win. They did not yet realize how great a contempt the Yankees had for any race but their own, how it would make us people with darker skins outcasts in our own land. It was Mexico, of course, and its corrupt government, that made many *Californios* yearn for something new. In particular, it was that pig, *General de Santa Ana, Presidente de Mexico*, and those who came after him, robbing us, when they even bothered to notice we existed. Ah, free Mexico. What a happy land after she threw out the Spaniards. War, corruption, repression. We

*Californios* wanted no part of it; we have always been free men, and the Mexicans used us, took from us, gave us nothing back. And for a while, after the Yankees arrived, it was very good. With so many men in the mines in the north, they needed our cattle, the food we raised. Our rancheros became very prosperous, and in that prosperity lay the seeds of our defeat, because these were not men used to money. They spent lavishly, gambled, and most of all, borrowed money. Then the mines closed, the floods came, killing so many animals, and after that the droughts burned us up, followed by a plague of grasshoppers. And smallpox to thin our numbers. Ah, señor, with so many debts and no more income, the old ranchos were lost. Not only the ranchos of we *Californios*, but also of Yankees, men like Don Able Stearns, who had come to California long ago, when the place was still Spanish, married a Spanish girl, accumulated much land. All of them, ruined."

Jorge chewed his lip for a moment. "Except for Don Andres. Our isolation saved us. Too far to market. We did not grow too quickly, so we did not borrow. Yes, we lost a great deal of cattle in the floods and droughts, but Don Andres is a wise and careful man. He has been rebuilding the herds. If we are not molested, all will be well again. Why not?" he added with a laugh. "Do we not now have five hundred American dollars?"

# CHAPTER SIX

The valley began to narrow. As the air grew fresher, there was a slight iodine flavor to each breath. "The sea," Gabe said to Jorge.

Jorge nodded. "Yes. Just a couple of miles away." He smiled. "You seem fascinated by the sea. You've mentioned it before, and always your eyes light up."

Gabe laughed. "It does fascinate me. I was born about as far from the sea as you can get, but even there I heard about it, the Great Water far to the west. Some of my people, before I was born, had gone to the Pacific, but way north of here. There were many stories in the village about the men and women who had made that trip. What a fantastic journey it must have been, through lands full of unknown people, strange customs. . . ."

"Well, now it'll be your turn to tell stories when you go back," Jorge replied. He immediately noticed the slight tightening of the muscles around Gabe's eyes and mouth and wished he'd not spoken. Gabe had little to go back to. The thought saddened Jorge, because his own world was shrinking, too, with nothing left of it but the difficult old man who was his *patrón*, and El Rancho de Las Palomas. And how long would either of them last?

"What's that?" Gabe asked, cutting into Jorge's thoughts. He'd seen red tile roofs ahead and what looked like bell towers. "I didn't think there were any towns in this part of the state."

"It's not a town," Jorge replied. "It's one of the missions . . . San Juan Capistrano. We'll be stopping there for a while. I think you will find it a beautiful place."

Gabe did find the mission beautiful, especially the gardens. The Franciscans, when they had come from Spain, most of them from the Balearic Islands in the Mediterranean, had brought with them many Mediterranean plants: pepper trees, oleanders, olives, grape vines, and many different kinds of shrubs and bamboo. All of these plants had thrived in the dry, mostly sunny Mediterranean, and here they had found a similar climate and once again thrived.

Gabe wandered through the gardens. An oasis of peace. There was peace inside the buildings, too, but a slightly forbidding peace; thick, whitewashed walls, dark, heavy wooden beams overhead, and everywhere symbols of suffering and death, men nailed to crosses, paintings of weeping women, other men with arrows protruding from their naked, bleeding bodies, while their eyes were raised to heaven in a kind of orgasmic agony. Even the name of the mission followed the same theme—San Juan Capistrano. Saint John the Beheaded. Not Gabe's idea of the Spirit World at all. But out in the garden, surrounded by the musky odor of the sage and flowers, the sharp tang of the pepper trees, he felt at home, part of a living world.

The resident Franciscan Brothers, in their brown robes, both simple and elegant, tended to Don Andres's wound. He seemed to know all of the brothers quite well. He decided to stay the night; obviously he felt comfortable here.

But Gabe did not feel like staying within four walls. He could smell the sea, not far away. "I'll be back in the morning," he told Jorge.

"Ah yes," Jorge said, smiling. "Your ocean obsession again. Well, if you must go, head straight west. Then, when your only other choice is to get wet, turn south for a couple of miles, and I think you'll find something you'll like very much."

Gabe nodded, mounted, and rode away from the mission, travelling alongside a riverbed, which was almost completely dry, yet willows and alders still grew in bursts of bright green, packed so thickly together that it was not possible to push a horse through them. Given any moisture at all, this land seemed to blossom.

Gabe reached the sea quite easily. It was late afternoon. The brassy glitter of sunlight reflected off the water into his eyes. He turned south. The trail climbed. Now he could look far out to sea, to a distant horizon, straight as a ruler. He continued to follow the trail until Jorge's promise came into view, a canyon, debouching from the barren hills to the east, breaking the line of bluffs, so that he was able to ride right down to the water, to a small cove, with a beach of glistening white sand, pure, untainted by civilization.

His horse was a little alarmed by the waves, which crashed onto the sand with considerable force. He staked the animal out in a patch of alders and mesquite a hundred yards back from the water. Taking his bedroll and saddlebags, he made a small camp right on the sand.

He was hungry, but not for the canned beans and bacon in his saddlebags. He drew out a length of line, then dug deeper into the saddlebags, yelping a little as a fish hook snagged his finger. He freed the hook, sucked his finger for a moment, then attached the hook to the line.

He eyed the surging surf with considerable misgivings, then decided on a spot where the canyon sides rose away from the beach and a low bluff overlooked the water. There was a spot low down on the bluff which he was sure he could reach.

He'd have to have some kind of bait. He considered opening a can of beans and bacon, but decided the force of the waves would wash anything like that right off the hook. Then, as his eyes were drawn toward the surf, he thought he saw movement against the sand. He ran over. Nothing. Then, as another wave rolled in and sagged back, he saw it again . . . small creatures frantically boring into the wet sand.

It took a few tries, but in five minutes he had a handful of ugly little creatures, some of them about an inch long, with lots of legs and soft grey shells. They'd stay on the hook.

With several of the creatures wrapped in his bandanna, he went up onto the bluff, then slid down to the little ledge that hung right over the water. He quickly skewered one of the sand creatures onto the hook, then tossed hook and bait into the water.

The waves surged and foamed just below him. He'd have to be careful not to fall. He almost did when two minutes later something took the hook, surprising him.

It was a good-sized hook and a stout line, so he had no trouble dragging the fish out of the water. It was a perch, weighing perhaps two pounds. He killed it with his knife, then went back to fishing. Within fifteen minutes, he had caught two more.

Returning to the beach, he built a small pit, using smooth beach stones. He filled the pit with driftwood that had been pushed up to the high tide mark. The wood was very dry. He soon had a hot, almost smokeless fire burning brightly. Going back into the brush, he cut small limbs on which to spit the fish. First he cleaned all three fish, while keeping an eye on the fire, which was quickly burning down to a bed of coals. He shoved the sticks through the fish and roasted them over the coals, adding small pieces of wood from time to time. The odor of the cooking fish overpowered him; he burnt himself eating chunks of the steaming white meat before it had cooled adequately.

He ate two of the fish and left one, already cooked, for breakfast. By now, the sun was setting. He watched it touch the horizon, watched the big red ball begin to dip out of sight. Slowly the horizon, which was layered with thin clouds, began to glow. Within a few minutes, Gabe was gazing in awe at the most amazing display of sunset colors he'd ever seen; streaks of orange, yellow, and lavender.

After checking his horse, he gathered some brush and used it to make a mat to protect his rifles from the sand.

As usual, he wanted both rifles within easy reach. Satisfied, he stretched his bedroll out onto the sand, took off his boots, trousers, and shirt, and slid into his bedding. Stars were beginning to appear, faded a little by a half-moon, which lay directly overhead. The wind had died to almost nothing, so that the waves rose smooth and sheer, and just before they broke, the moon's soft light was reflected back at him from the glassy walls of water in a million glittering fragments.

He lay on his back, drowsing, hypnotized by the surf, amazed by how many different sounds it made: the crash of a wave into shallower water, the soft sound of the retreating wave as it slid over the sand, an occasional hollow boom as a wave collapsed on air trapped inside it. A constant, soothing murmur that soon put him to sleep.

He woke once, not sure of what time it was, not caring. The moon was waning. A silvery, ghostly track shone on the water, directly from the moon straight to Gabe. He fell asleep again, waking hours later to spray-misted daylight.

He got up at once. First he stowed his gear, putting it into place on his horse. Barefooted, he walked into the water. Damn! It was colder than it looked!

Gabe ate the remaining fish, then mounted. He tried to get his horse to run in the surf—he'd heard that it was good for a horse's legs—but the big stallion, eyes rolling, was not about to have anything to do with all that crashing water.

It was time to head back to the mission. He was a little late; he met Don Andres and Jorge just setting out. The rest of Juan's men had already headed back. Jorge would be driving the wagon. Both his and Don Andres's horses trailed along behind, attached to the wagon by long lead ropes.

The old man looked much better. He'd propped himself up against his saddle, which lay in the back of the wagon. "Jorge tells me you went to see the ocean," he said to Gabe.

Gabe nodded. He said nothing about his night by the water; its magic belonged to him personally, it was his own possession, to hold onto. Don Andres seemed to understand.

Jorge, a little miffed at being demoted from horseman to wagon driver, got into the driver's seat and flicked the reins at the two nags drawing the wagon. Grudgingly, they leaned into the harness, and the wagon began to roll.

Gabe rode close to the wagon. Jorge, talkative, gestured to the area around them. "About ten years ago there was a lot of killing near here," he said, conversationally. "A man named Juan Flores got tired of the way the Yankees were treating him. There was a particularly brutal sheriff. When Juan could take no more, he started to fight back. This sheriff, he got himself a posse and came after Juan. Flores had a lot of men with him. They ambushed the sheriff and his posse and killed most of them, including the sheriff."

Don Andres, who had been listening, snorted angrily. "Flores! That *hijo de puta*! All he managed to do was bring down a lot of Yankee vengeance on innocent people, *Californios* who'd had nothing to do with Flores and his gang of loafers, but the Yankees killed anyone who didn't look Anglo."

Jorge grinned. Gabe began to get the idea that he was needling Don Andres as revenge for wagon duty "There was a little more to it than that," Jorge said to Gabe. "Flores, after he killed all those Yankees, began to think of himself as a general. And everyone knows that generals need money, so he started extorting money from remote ranches."

Jorge shot a quick look at Don Andres, perhaps to judge the old man's reactions, to see how far he could go. Don Andres was staring stonily ahead. Jorge continued. "Flores tried to extort money from El Rancho de Las Palomas." He looked quickly at Don Andres again, then smiled. "I think that was a decision Flores later regretted very much."

Don Andres snorted a second time, but Gabe thought he could see a pleased gleam in the old man's eyes. "Hah! Those bandits left with a lot of our lead in their miserable hides."

Both Gabe and Jorge grinned. Memories of days past, of action and danger overcome, seemed to agree with Don Andres. He lay back against his saddle, smiling.

No one said much for the next few hours. The trail took them south along the coast. Gabe spent most of his time studying the various colors of the ocean, big swirls of differing shades of blue, and always, in the distance, that sharp horizon line. The temperature was slightly on the brisk side. Around midday, a wind kicked up, and with the water's surface disturbed, the ocean changed its appearance once again, its color softening to a deep blue, almost a purple.

That afternoon they finally turned away from the sea, heading up a broad valley, alongside a shallow river with luxuriant vegetation covering its banks. About five miles inland they came to another mission, but unlike San Juan Capistrano, this mission was in ruins. Don Andres sighed bitterly as they passed crumbling bell towers and ruined adobe walls, lots of them. Gabe figured it had been a big place. "Mission San Luis Rey de Francia," Don Andres told Gabe. "It used to be called the King of the Missions. Thousands of cattle, horses, dozens of Indian novitiates. Then that damned government in Mexico, in its infinite wisdom, let the sharks have it. They left only bones."

They camped for the night further up the valley. This far from the sea, it was much warmer, except at night, which was beginning to take on a chill. They were on the trail again shortly after dawn, beginning to climb into foothills. Much higher mountains lay ahead. They cut south, through a small valley. At times they passed small farms and ranches, but they did not stop; Don Andres seemed in a hurry to reach home, as if his strength lay there, as if he were afraid that he might waste away unless he reached it quickly.

In the late afternoon they passed through a broad valley. Don Andres abruptly sat up straight and pointed to a gentle slope that rose to the left of the trail. "That's where we fought them," he told Gabe. "Fought them and beat them . . . the Americanos. After they came out of the desert. They were tired, frightened, and we were there, waiting for them. They were mounted men, they called themselves dragoons, but we were *Californios*, we were men who'd been born on the back of a horse, and they were only hired soldiers. They were foolish, they did not study the lay of the land, and we charged them, charged with our lances, and we beat them. Only our decency kept us from wiping them out completely; when we saw how badly they were hurt, how many men they had lost, we let the survivors ride away."

Gabe read the fierce pride on the old man's face as he remembered his day of glory. Then Don Andres sighed. "It was the only time we beat them in an open fight. We lost everything else. But . . . that day . . . that one day was glorious."

They camped one more night on the trail. In the morning, when they started out again, Don Andres was clearly growing tired of sitting in the wagon. He fretted for the next three hours, as the trail rose higher and higher into the mountains. The horses were blowing hard by the time they reached the top of the pass up which they'd been laboring for the past several miles. Just before starting down the other side, the horses stopped, as if for the view.

And quite a view it was. A broad valley lay below, an expanse of rich, rolling land, with thick stands of trees indicating where water ran. Mountains rose all around, as if protecting the valley. Gabe could see cattle, clumps of them, moving below in small groups, and further to the northeast there was more green, and a suggestion of long, low buildings.

Both Jorge and Don Andres sat motionless in the wagon, looking at the beautiful valley that lay stretched out before them. Gabe could read the love in their eyes, love of land, love of home. He was not surprised when Jorge finally turned to him and said, "There it is, señor. The place we have been talking about, the place where we live."

His voice dropped a little. When he spoke again, it was in a half whisper. "El Rancho de Las Palomas."

# CHAPTER SEVEN

Don Andres insisted on mounting his horse for the ride into the ranch. "I will not arrive in this wagon," he insisted, "like a sick old lady."

His horse was untied from the wagon, which did not please the horse; it had been happy enough not to have any weight on its back. The animal was saddled, and Don Andres managed to mount with only minimal help.

It was only about a mile to the ranch buildings. Don Andres sat his big white stallion proudly, straight in the saddle. As far as Gabe could see, he showed no signs of his wound.

They were spotted before they'd gotten halfway there. Three riders, herding a small group of cattle, broke away and came galloping in their direction. Gabe was impressed by the loose, wild, easy way they rode. Don Andres had been right; these were men born on horseback.

Shouted greetings were called out. Don Andres answered with a regal wave of his right hand, still looking straight ahead, toward the headquarters of his domain. The riders peeled off again, raced down to the adobes ahead of Don Andres, shouting out the news.

When they arrived, people were spilling out of buildings, or if already outside, dropping their work, everyone running toward Don Andres, who was still cantering along proudly

on his white horse. Gabe followed a little behind. Jorge was
about fifty yards back of Gabe, obviously quite disgruntled
about riding up in a rickety wagon.

Gabe took the opportunity to study the scene around him.
People. Lots of them, men, women, children. This was obviously an operation meant to support human beings, depend-
ents, very different from the sparsely manned Anglo ranches
Gabe had visited, where the sole purpose was money, profit,
with as few employees to feed and pay as possible. On that
kind of ranch, that's what people were—employees, rather
than an integral part of the ranch. And highly expendable.

Not here, not at El Rancho de Las Palomas. It was
a rather messy scene: animal pens placed haphazardly,
barking dogs, children, chickens squawking in alarm at
all the activity, women cooking in outdoor kitchens. There
seemed to be saddled horses posted everywhere, ready to
ride. None of them looked in very good shape.

After discounting the obvious differences, Gabe decided that El Rancho de Las Palomas reminded him of an
Oglala village, the constant activity, the sense of people
busily living out their daily lives. The biggest difference,
of course, was that unlike an Oglala village, this one could
not be packed up and moved. Here it was, here it would
stay . . . as long as men like Barnes did not get their hands
on it. Gabe had an image of Barnes riding into this valley
and immediately dispossessing ninety percent of the people
who now lived here. For the sake of efficiency. Profit—the
White Man's god.

Someone had taken the reins of Don Andres's horse. The
old man now dismounted, fairly gracefully, Gabe noticed,
although he was aware of the pinched look of pain on
Don Andres's face. Others noticed it, too, then noticed the
bloody bandage around his waist. A gabble of wild talking
and shouting ensued, as everyone started asking questions.
Of course, all eyes were on Gabe, the Americano with the
long hair and pale eyes. Had this man been a party to
wounding their lord and master?

By now the wagon had reached the yard. Jorge jumped
down onto the hard-packed, dirty ground. Gabe noticed

that his eyes were roaming over the assembled crowd, expectantly. Gabe heard a glad cry, and a woman left one of the kitchens and came running toward Jorge. Gabe watched them come together, embrace, laugh, speak to each other.

Gabe was impressed. He had not realized that Jorge had such a pretty wife. Pretty? No, she was beautiful. And young, much younger than Jorge, perhaps no more than twenty. In size, she was perhaps a little more than medium height, with long, dark hair, falling over her shoulders in a thick, shining mass. Her body was slender, but rounded in all the right places, her hips full under her long skirt. Her low-cut cotton blouse, scooped off the shoulders, left little to imagine about her breasts, which were large and well-shaped. But it was her face that drew most of Gabe's attention, a lovely face, with well-defined features, dominated by a pair of large, dark eyes which at the moment were flashing with delight. The girl seemed to shine with uninhibited aliveness.

Gabe felt a little left out. He had not been close to a woman for some time and missed a woman's warmth. Unfortunately, Jorge's wife, with her dark hair and huge eyes, reminded him too much of his Oglala wife, Yellow Buckskin Girl. Who was dead. But he must not think of that, must not dwell again on the terrible image of the bullet entering her forehead, blowing her head apart, while he watched from a distance, helpless to save her. But the image came nevertheless, and as he relived its horror the same cold, killing rage swept over him, as it had when he'd seen it happen, a rage mixed with a horrible sense of loss. He'd avenged her; he'd killed the man who'd killed Yellow Buckskin Girl, killed him horribly. But, as necessary as the vengeance had been, it had not brought her back to him.

Gabe dismounted and tied his horse to a hitching rack. There seemed to be hitching racks everywhere, most of them tenanted by tired-looking, saddled nags. He was wondering what to do about his gear when Jorge turned and saw him. His face lit up. He turned to the girl and said something, and then they were both coming toward Gabe, who turned to meet them.

"Gabe," Jorge said happily, "I would like you to meet my sister, Mercedes."

Sister? Gabe found himself looking at the girl with much greater interest, only to find her appraising him just as carefully. For a moment their eyes met and held, a very long moment, although Gabe had no idea of its real duration. Then Jorge spoke, although Gabe was unaware of the actual words, and Gabe felt released, able to look away, although he did not really want to. Something had passed between himself and this girl, Mercedes. He'd felt it in his gut, and he knew, he was positive, that she'd felt it, too.

Careful, careful, careful, he warned himself. This is your friend's sister. He had by now begun to think of Jorge as a friend, and he knew how protective Spanish men were of their women. Hands off, eyes off, think of something else.

Jorge was helping. "Gabe, I want you to meet my family, my wife, my sons." He was already leading the way toward a small group that could be nothing except a family, a plump, quiet-looking woman in her thirties, surrounded by a gaggle of children of various ages. So far, no mention of daughters, although Gabe could see girls among the children clustered around the woman. But sons, well . . .

Gabe trailed after Jorge, turning once to look back at Mercedes. What a beautiful name. As he turned, he discovered she was still looking at him. Once again their eyes met, and once again it was nearly impossible to look away. He felt that through her eyes he was looking straight into her, and he liked what he saw.

He tore himself away, went through five minutes of confusing introductions to Jorge's wife, children, cousins, an uncle, even a very old man, who appeared to be an Indian, whom Jorge introduced as his grandfather. But each new face was vague to Gabe, overlayed by beautiful, soft features dominated by a pair of the most amazing eyes. Stop it! he warned himself again.

He forced himself to pay attention to what was happening around him. By now, the story of the gunfight against Barnes's hired killers had been told at least half a dozen times. Gabe received many approving looks from the

assembled vaqueros, as the man who'd stood beside their
*patrón*. Bloodthirsty promises of vengeance against Barnes
and company flew thick and fast, idle threats, because
Barnes was far away, but Gabe was already familiar with
Latin machismo and knew that this boasting made the men
feel less guilty that they had not been there to help.

Don Andres was obviously tiring. Jorge finally noticed
and waved two old women forward. They led Don Andres
into the biggest of the adobes to dress his wound. And now
Jorge turned to Gabe. "Come with me," he said. "You will
want a place to put your gear."

Gabe nodded. It had been a long ride. He was tired of sitting a saddle; his buttocks and legs ached. It would be nice to
rest for a while, best of all, to take a bath. He was surprised,
however, when Jorge led him into the main house, the one
into which Don Andres had disappeared. Jorge was aware of
his surprise.

"Don't worry," he said, laughing. "It is a big house, with
lots of room. The señora, Don Andres's wife, died three
years ago. He likes having people near him."

The house, two massive stories of adobe, appeared to be at
least sixty or seventy years old. Inside, they passed through
a large living room with dark beams overhead. Tiles, well-
polished by generations of boots, covered the floor. Looking
through the window openings, Gabe could see that the walls
were at least three feet thick. The furniture was sparse, most
of it made of heavy, dark wood. An occasional crucifix or
saint's picture decorated the whitewashed walls.

Gabe was shown into a room at the back of the
house. It was large, and because of the whitewashed
walls, quite bright. There was a simple wood-framed
bed, with rawhide strips lashed across the framing. A
thin mattress lay on top of the webbing. The single
window looked out of the rear of the house, toward
a stand of trees about forty yards away. A massive
wooden bureau stood against one wall, and in a corner there was a wooden washstand holding an enamel
washbowl. Simple but adequate, a good place to spend
the night.

Two men had followed them inside, carrying Gabe's gear, a courtesy of the house toward a man who had already served it well. I guess that means I've got status, Gabe thought. He'd already noticed that Don Andres never carried anything, not even the smallest package. When he'd commented on it to Jorge, the *capataz* had been surprised that the question had even been asked. "But of course! A *caballero*, a *gente de razon*, would never actually carry anything, like a common workman!"

Custom. And not as senseless as it sounded. Gabe knew where this particular custom had come from, and when. The conquest of Mexico. From even before that, during the wars in Spain against the Moors. When he'd been with his grandfather in Boston, he'd read every book he could get his hands on. Particularly books that would explain to him the strange new white culture in which he suddenly found himself. He especially enjoyed history books. He'd read about the Spaniards who had conquered Mexico. They had been of the Spanish warrior class, men who had to be ready to fight at any time, and no warrior who wants to survive will burden his hands with anything other than weapons. It had been the same among the Oglala. A man's life was to fight. A woman's life was to carry. Just as it should be among a warrior people.

When Gabe had seen his gear deposited in the room, he started back outside. Jorge seemed a little surprised. "But, would you not like to rest for a while? It's been a long ride."

"My horse," Gabe explained. "It's still saddled. I have to make sure . . ."

"Ah," Jorge replied, shrugging away the subject. "It's only a horse, and horses can wait."

Gabe hesitated. He knew how little the old *Californios* thought of horses; they were viewed as convenient machines, to be used hard, then discarded. Gabe had no foolish ideas about horses; they were often ornery creatures, and finicky as hell. But in the kind of life he led, having a good horse in good shape could often mean the difference between survival and death. Probably the same held true for the *Californios*, too, but as Jorge had told him, in the old days they had literally thousands of horses, indeed, had to kill many of them off in dry years, when there was little forage. So, they used them hard and threw them away when they collapsed.

He'd heard Anglo horsemen complain about Latin horse gear, especially ring bits, which could easily break a horse's jaw. And of the long, cruel, Spanish rowels, which lacerated a horse's flanks. None of that for Gabe. He had one good horse and he expected it to serve him well . . . as long as he took good care of it. He would have to make sure that he looked after the animal's welfare himself.

Jorge shrugged off Gabe's peculiar behavior, although he was a little embarrassed for his friend as he personally unsaddled the animal, rubbed it down, then turned it into a corral, rather than having one of the vaqueros do it for him. But, everyone knew that Americanos were people with strange habits.

Half an hour later, a huge dinner was served. Gabe had seen women bending over huge iron and earthen pots. It was easy to watch them cook, because the kitchens were outside, open to the weather, except for flimsy tile roofs to keep off the rain. If it ever did rain here.

Gabe would have liked to take a bath before dinner, but there did not seem to be a bathroom, so he filled the basin in his room from a pitcher, then sponged himself down.

Since the weather was nice, dinner took place outside, everyone eating together at big, rough plank tables. Gabe sat at the main table, with Don Andres, Jorge, Mercedes, and with others who had sufficient status. The food was phenomenal: big chunks of beef, swimming in chili sauce; tamales, stuffed with meat and more chili sauce; huge, soft, handmade tortillas. Gabe had watched the women patting them out by hand. And beans, of course, served hot and spicy, from big iron frying pans. Don Andres drank wine. "From my own vineyards," he told Gabe, with not a little pride, while Jorge and Mercedes drank a somewhat green beer, also made on the property. Gabe drank a *refresco*, made of water and crushed wild berries.

He noticed that most of the people gathered around the tables were of mixed blood, with Don Andres at one extreme, apparently pure Spanish, and several of the older working people, pure Indian, or close to it. A handsome slice of humanity, generally olive in color, with glossy black hair, a people full of life, glowing with health, probably because of their diet, rich in meat, and hard, outdoor work. Gabe liked them.

The conversation at dinner was quite animated. He took part as best he could, although many comments passed over his head, having to do with life on the ranch, events that had happened or should happen. But, listening to Don Andres and Jorge, one particular vein of conversation began to seep through to him. They expected him to stay, to become a part of El Rancho de Las Palomas. They spoke of the matter as if it were the only natural conclusion to what had happened so far.

Gabe did not know how to reply. Stay? In one place? From boyhood, he'd been brought up among a people who moved frequently, packing up their entire village, loading their lodges and robes onto travois, and riding away. Stay? Gabe did not know if he would ever be able to do that. He'd intended only to see Don Andres safe at home, then ride away to see what else he could discover about this land where winter never happened.

However, as he looked around the table at the friendly faces surrounding him, saw the way they interacted as a group, he was once again reminded of an Oglala village. An organic whole. Perhaps, for just a little while . . .

He looked across the table, toward Mercedes, a mistake if he wanted peace of mind, because she looked up at the same moment, and once again their eyes met. She did not exactly smile, her expression was even a little grave, as if she were pondering some mystery, and again he felt something pass between them. Something . . . fascinating. Perhaps even a little disturbing.

Still looking into those huge, dark eyes, he decided, why not? Why not stay just a little while longer? A few days.

And then, back into those eyes, and the thought came, unbidden, dangerous, frightening: Why not stay for a lifetime?

# CHAPTER EIGHT

The rider galloped closer, his horse's hooves scattering dust and clods of dirt. Suddenly the rider bent low on the right side of his mount, down and down, until it seemed as if he would certainly fall. His right hand pawed at the dirt, then he was erect in the saddle again, holding aloft for all to see the coin he'd scooped up at a full gallop. Loud cheering greeted his feat.

Yes, Gabe admitted, these *Californios* could definitely ride. The finest Oglala brave could ride no better.

It was five days since they'd arrived at the ranch. Five days to let Don Andres's wound heal a little, then the Latin desire for a fiesta could no longer be denied. The women had been cooking since the day before. Huge haunches of beef were roasting over open fires, stew pots bubbled, spreading wonderful aromas of meat, beans, and chilies. Children ran everywhere, half crazy with anticipatory excitement.

Then there were the men, strutting, preparing equipment, bragging about what mighty feats they would accomplish. And they were accomplishing them. A race course had been laid out about two hundred yards from the house. Big trestle tables had been set up nearby, so the onlookers could eat and drink while they watched. Don Andres had been installed in a big wooden chair behind one of the smaller tables. Jorge

sat to one side of him, Mercedes on the other. Gabe sat at a
larger table, a little ways distant.

The first event had already been run, a race around the
course, with the riders required to hold coins between their
thighs and the saddle. The man who finished first, with all
the coins still in place, won.

Now, picking up coins at the gallop. About half the men
had been successful. Men swaggered, their victory smiles
showing the white gleam of teeth against mahogany skin.

Gabe noticed that a number of interested looks were coming his way. He was the new man, the favored. But what had
he done so far, except save the *patrón's* life? Could he ride?
That was the question Gabe saw on the face of every man
there, and on the faces of half the women.

Including Mercedes. She had not made a production of it,
but he knew she was wondering. If a man could not ride, a
man was not really a man.

Gabe's horse was standing, saddled, a few yards away. He
had ridden over from the house; all the men had ridden. In
this part of the world, if a man had only fifty yards to travel, he would still mount a horse for the trip. Only the lowest
peasant walked.

Feeling a little like a kid, knowing he was doing this for a
woman he could never even touch, Gabe walked over to his
horse. He waited while a rider made a pass at the coins. And
missed. Gabe could see two or three coins shining against
the dirt.

He mounted. A murmur went up from the crowd. Gabe
slowly cantered toward the far end of the course. His horse
pranced sideways, snorting; it had not been ridden much lately. He hoped it would not give him trouble.

When he reached the end of the course, he turned his
mount and immediately slammed his heels against its ribs.
The animal reared; Gabe knew it was an impressive sight,
that big black stallion pawing the air, its nostrils flaring, its
eyes wide. Then the horse broke into a dead run.

Halfway through the course, Gabe glanced at the crowd.
At one person in particular. Mercedes. She was watching
him, but she saw him looking at her and casually looked

away. A feeling of loss swept over him, then he jerked his mind back onto what he was doing. The coins were just ahead; he was going to miss them if he didn't stop acting like a boy who'd just seen his first love.

He was aware of the smooth rippling of his muscles as he bent low, upper body relaxed, his fingers closing unerringly around not one, but two of the coins, a gamble, because he could have easily dropped both, but he did not. A moment later he was riding his horse past the crowd, a coin in each hand, and as he passed by, he noticed, with a glad thumping of his heart, that Mercedes was looking straight at him, and her eyes were shining with excitement.

The crowd roared a loud "Olé!" as Gabe cantered up to Don Andres's table. He bent from the saddle, gently laying both coins on the tabletop. Don Andres nodded graciously, although his eyes were full of pain as he silently cursed the wound that kept him from riding alongside his vaqueros.

When Gabe dismounted he was treated to a great deal of backslapping from the men, and hot glances from a few of the women. The unmarried ones. He half-turned and saw that Mercedes was watching him. To his surprise, her expression was intense, almost hostile. Then he realized why. It was the women around him, the attention they were paying him. My God, he thought, she's actually jealous!

He felt wonderful. Someone thrust a big chunk of roasted meat into Gabe's hand. He slowly ate it as he led his horse back to a hitching rail. Juice ran down his chin. He was feeling better than he'd felt in a long time. These people knew how to live—plenty of work, but plenty of play, too. He did not regret that he had finally given in to Jorge's urging that he stay for at least the fiesta.

The next event was beginning. The *Carrera del Gallo*. The Race of the Cock. Men were already burying angry roosters up to their necks in soft dirt. One man drew back a pecked hand, sucking away blood, laughing.

When several roosters had been buried, the runs started, riders pounding down toward where the nervous birds had been interred. The point was to seize them by the head and pull them out of the ground, but the heads of the roosters were darting this way and that, a much more difficult target than an inert coin.

The first man missed. A groan of disappointment rose from the crowd. The man rode slowly back toward the start, his head low.

The next man got his bird. Racing by at a full gallop, he successfully seized its head and neck. The rooster came out of the ground in a shower of dirt and feathers, squawking loudly. The proud victor rode his horse in a big circle, displaying his struggling captive.

There seemed to be an altercation down by the start. Gabe and everyone else turned in that direction. It was a third man's turn, but the man who'd failed in his first try was insisting that he be given the chance to try again. The other man, eager to have his own chance, was protesting. The problem was solved when the man who'd failed pushed the other man out of his saddle, then put spurs to his horse and came thundering down the course on his second run. Gabe saw the look of ferocious intensity on the man's face as he leaned out of his saddle, reaching for the rooster's darting, snaking head. The man's hand closed around it, he straightened in the saddle, but the bird had been too deeply buried, and the head came off in the rider's hand. Blood spurted, and the man looked at the mess in his hand and angrily threw the head away from him.

The crowd, however, was enthusiastic. Their loud cheering brought a big smile to the man's face, and he cavorted his mount for several seconds, before finally riding away.

Gabe was amused. How like Oglala warriors, he thought. All balls and brass, with tempers as fragile as a child's. More and more he was feeling at home. If only these *Californios* had the ability to travel as a band.

People were calling out to Gabe, encouraging him to take part in the *Carrera del Gallo*, but by now it was too late; the last of the birds had either been plucked from the ground or lost their heads. Yet Gabe wanted to ride, was full of excitement, eagerness. Maybe he could show them something from his own people.

Without saying a word, he picked up a block of wood a little larger than a man's head and set it down on a stump, off to one side of the course. He then pulled out his pistol and checked the loads. He was wearing only the one pistol, on his right hip, butt forward as usual; he'd left off the shoulder rig. The crowd fell silent, watching him as he spun the Remington's cylinder, checking that the caps were tightly in place, the chamber mouths well-greased. Gabe had already noticed that pistols were not common-place among the *Californios*; they tended toward edged weapons: lances, knives, and a short heavy sword some of the vaqueros carried at the side of their saddle, under their left leg.

Gabe holstered the pistol, mounted his horse, and can-tered slowly toward the starting position. He passed Mercedes along the way, glanced at her sideways, saw her meet his look boldly. Jorge was standing near the girl. He caught the look they exchanged. Gabe saw an expression of amazed awareness come over the *capataz's* face, as he looked from his sister to Gabe and back at his sister again.

Gabe clamped his lips tightly shut. Now he'd gone and done it. He'd insulted Jorge. What he did not see was the delighted smile that creased Jorge's features after Gabe had ridden by.

Seething, Gabe made the turn, then once again urged his horse into a gallop. He pulled the pistol from its holster, cranked back the hammer. A murmur came from the crowd, but not too much of a murmur. After all, he was clearly going to shoot at the block of wood on the stump as he galloped by. Impressive, but not all that impressive; there were many men at El Rancho de Las Palomas who could easily do the same.

They were not prepared when Gabe slid off the far side of his horse, nearly disappearing from view behind the animal's big body. Almost the only part of him visible was his left heel, hooked over the saddle. Then everyone saw the muzzle of the pistol appear beneath the horse's neck.

By now, Gabe was concentrating far too hard to worry about the crowd, or Jorge, or Mercedes. First, he had to keep from falling. Then he had to hit the block. And while he was trying to hit the block, he had to make sure the pistol was far enough away from his horse's neck to keep the muzzle blast from singing its hide.

He could not aim; he could barely see the target. He lined up the muzzle by feel, then pressed the trigger. The pistol roared. Chips flew from the block; it spun around once, then fell from the stump.

A great shout went up from the onlookers. Especially from the men. It was not just the accuracy of the shot, made under difficult conditions, but also Gabe's horsemanship. Always horsemanship. The fact that the stallion had not flinched when Gabe fired from directly beneath its neck was a tribute to his control over the animal.

When he rode past the crowd again, he was aware of Mercedes's eyes shining in his direction. He caught her gaze for a moment, then hurriedly looked away; he'd done enough damage for one day. He was only barely aware of a moment's hurt on her face, and then he was by.

By now, hunger was drawing even the boldest of the men toward the big trestle tables that sagged beneath mammoth loads of food. Gabe tied his horse nearby, then joined the men at one of the tables. He was treated to a number of rough slaps on the back, big smiles, but, he realized, still rather tentative smiles. He was, after all, a new man in a society where most members had been born on the premises. Furthermore, he was of another culture. Or was that two cultures? His past was just another complication for the people around him, all of them prisoners of rigid tradition, to try and figure out.

However, wine soon loosened inhibitions. Gabe watched, impressed, as the men around him, and many of the women, poured vast quantities of wine, beer, and brandy down their throats. Amazingly, most of the drinkers merely became more boisterous, friendly, happy. He compared it to what alcohol had done to his people, how it had completely altered their characters, so that a man might kill his best friend in a sudden drunken rage, or sell his wife or daughter for more alcohol.

Gabe realized that most of the men at his table were older. He listened to them carefully; the old could tell him things about this new world that the young had never bothered to think about. One old man interested him in particular. Gabe had already noticed that he did not appear to be of mixed blood, or if so, very lightly mixed; he looked all Spanish.

The old man, who's name was Miguel, hastened to verify Gabe's impression. He was obviously proud of his heritage. "My grandfather and grandmother came to California with the first group of settlers," Miguel said. There were slight sighs of resignation from the men around him; obviously they were about to hear once again a story already told many times.

"They came from Mallorca, with the Founder himself. With Junípero Serra. And Crespi. Fine men, men of God. And with Portolá. My grandfather was one of *Capitan* Portolá's soldiers for a while . . . until he got himself some land. Oh, those must have been the days, señor. This vast land, empty except for a few savages, and those fine men of Mallorca and Menorca, bringing God's light to those who had never seen light, to those who lived in ignorance of God's mercy."

One of the other men poked Miguel in the ribs. "I never knew you to pay much attention to God or his priests, Miguel. What's happening? Getting old? Smelling the grave?"

Some of the men laughed. Miguel colored a little, then, after a big swig of wine, decided to laugh, too. "It's true, I suppose. I was always more interested in what life has given us here, this beautiful land, its mysteries. . . ."

"Mostly interested in those mysteries underneath a woman's skirts, if I remember correctly," another old codger broke in.

Miguel smiled quite willingly this time; his machismo had just been complimented. "God knows I fathered enough brats," he admitted. "Not that they turned out to be much. Forgetting the old ways. . . ."

"The old ways were hard, Miguel."

"True," Miguel admitted. "There was a new land to tame. But do you remember the freedom of it, Carlos? This land as it was then? Why, señor," he said, turning to Gabe, "there were never many of us, but we were here together, a light in this land. The hospitality. That's what I remember most. A man could ride from San Diego to Sonoma, a distance of two hundred leagues, and never would he go without food and shelter. All he had to do was stop at a ranch, a mission, even the poorest house, and his needs would be taken care of. Even horses. He would leave his horse and be lent a horse to use, for as long as he needed it. On his way back home, a traveler would drop off borrowed horse after borrowed horse, a chain of them. And if the horse was ridden to death, well, what could one say? What else is a horse for, but to serve mankind?"

"That's all we had," another man said. "Horses and cattle. That was our only wealth. We were too far from others of our kind. We were on our own. A simple life, few belongings, almost no money. . . ."

"Hides were our money," Miguel broke in. "The hides of all those hundreds of thousands of cattle. Leather. Tallow. Yet, unfortunately," he said to Gabe, "we could not trade them to others who shared our own roots, the people of Mexico and South America. There were too many deserts to cross, too many contrary winds for ships to make easy passage south to north. It was the Yankees who made some of us rich. Yankee traders in their clipper ships, who brought us so many things from the outside world that we could not provide for ourselves: tools, fine fabrics for clothing, lace mantillas for our women, metal, whiskey and rum. They brought us so many of these things, and some travelled all the way around the world before they reached us, because those ships came to California from China and the Philippines. And when they left, with their holds stuffed full of our hides and tallow, they sailed back to the eastern United States around the tip of South America. Brave men."

"Greedy men, too," another man said sourly. "They saw what we had here, saw our beautiful land, then sent an army not too many years later."

Glum silence. But Miguel was not about to be squelched. "Ah, the hide trade," he said jovially. "All those thousands of hides. And the tallow. Once a year, we would have a giant *matanza*, señor, a killing of cattle. Days of work, skinning the carcasses, cutting away the fat. The women rendering the fat down into tallow, the smell as it boiled in those big copper kettles. Then the women, bless their work, stacked the tallow onto the hides, and the men helped them tie each hide, with its tallow, into a big bundle. The *carretas* . . . remember their axles squealing, Carlos, as we took each of those big *botas* of tallow to the beach? And the stacks of cured hides, smelling pretty bad, ready to be taken out to those black Yankee clippers?"

Carlos nodded his head. "I remember. Especially the *nuqueo*. The excitement of it."

"Ah, God, yes, the *nuqueo*!" Miguel said excitedly. "How could I ever forget it! Thousands of animals down, and never any powder or ball wasted. How we could ride!"

Gabe looked puzzled. *Nuqueo*. He knew that *nuca* meant the nape of the neck. This *nuqueo* must have something to do with necks.

Miguel saw his confusion. "We stabbed them in the neck," he said. "Killed the cattle that way. One strong thrust with this, and they dropped in their tracks."

He took a long, pointed dagger from its sheath and held it up for Gabe to examine. "We would start out quietly," Miguel explained. "We would ride around a big herd, leaning out of the saddle to stab the cattle in the nape of the neck. Cattle are very stupid. Sometimes we were able to do this for quite a while, drop a lot of animals before the others would finally panic and run. Then we would ride after them, a mad dash of cattle, horses, and men, *nuqueandolos*, one after the other. They'd go down at a full run, ass over tail.

We'd kill thousands in a single day. And then the *peladores* would come, to skin the carcasses, and the women to strip the fat away and begin their work with the tallow."

"And all those carcasses?" Gabe asked.

Miguel shrugged. "We left most of them where they fell. Far too much meat for our small population. How happy the coyotes must have been! Of course, the *tasajearos* cut up some of the meat and dried it out for jerky. And we ate well each night. But . . . what could be done with so much meat?"

Gabe said nothing. He remembered similar scenes, from his boyhood, the men riding out from the village to hunt buffalo, and as the buffalo fell, the women following, each determining which animals her man had killed by the design on the feathers on the arrows sticking out of the animals' massive black sides. Then the skinning and the cutting up of meat and the following feasts. Later, the drying of meat to make pemmican. But they did not leave thousands of carcasses lying untouched. Life was too precious for that, the buffalo were the People's only wealth. However, the Spaniards had been doing it for money, for the cash and goods the sale of the hides would bring. To men of European stock, the gain of money seemed to justify just about anything. Even to these people.

Suddenly Miguel rose to his feet. He weaved a little, obviously more drunk than Gabe had suspected. "I'll show you," he said. "I'll show you how we used to do it. I'll show you the *nuqueo*."

Cries of drunken delight rose from around the table, as old Miguel wove a zigzag path toward his horse, which was tied up just a few yards away. Once mounted, however, his tipsiness seemed to vanish. He sat the saddle straight and alert, with a young man's grace.

A small pen lay about two hundred yards away, where a few cattle had been penned up, meat for the feast. Three animals remained, one of them a big rangy old steer, with wide sweeping horns. Miguel rode over to the pen, leaned down to open the gate, then, using the end of his reata, chased the steer out into the open.

The animal was already a little spooked by the noise and smell of the fiesta. It snorted, but held its ground. Miguel whacked the steer's haunch with his reata. It began to trot around in a small circle, growing more and more nervous by the second.

Others had begun to notice what was happening. Gabe saw Don Andres glance over from his table, frown in puzzlement, then smile when he realized what Miguel was trying to do.

Miguel let out a loud yell and whacked the steer again. With a bellow of anger and fear, the steer began to run . . . straight toward the fiesta.

Miguel clapped spurs to his horse's flanks and raced after the steer. As pursuer and pursued thundered down toward the tables, people began to scatter in alarm. Miguel let out another loud cry; his horse was closing the distance. Then he was alongside the steer. Gabe saw the flash of the heavy dagger in the old man's hand, saw him bend low, over the steer's neck. They were now only about thirty yards from the tables.

One hard, downward stroke, right into the nape of the steer's neck, and it was as if invisible supporting strings had been cut. The steer collapsed at a dead run, ass over teakettle, as Gabe had heard white men put it, dead before it hit the ground, a rolling wreckage of over half a ton of meat, crashing into one of the tables, scattering food, plates, and people.

Slowly, the dust settled. There was a moment's stunned silence, then Gabe heard his name being called.

He turned. Miguel was sitting his horse a few yards away, panting a little, a smile splitting his wrinkled old face from ear to ear. "And that, señor," he shouted, "is the way we used to do it! That is the *nuqueo*."

A great cheer went up from the crowd. The wrecked table, the near brush with disaster, were forgotten. When Miguel dismounted, he was escorted by a mob of happy, laughing men, the older among them swapping stories of the old days.

Gabe went back to his own table, which had been untouched by the near disaster. A few old men still sat around it, although some had gotten up to either congratulate Miguel or help those who had already begun to butcher the steer.

Gabe noticed that one of the old men was not smiling, but rather, looked down at his plate, his face grave. In appearance, he was the opposite of Miguel. If Miguel was all Spanish, this man was all Indian. Yet he wore the same clothing as the others, and spoke the same brand of Spanish. Gabe realized that he had heard this man utter very few words, while the others had talked so animatedly of the old days.

Seeing that no one was near enough to hear, Gabe turned to the old man. "Grandfather," he said, the way an Oglala might have said it, "what is troubling you?"

The old man looked up, straight into Gabe's eyes. He held the younger man's gaze steadily for several seconds, until something in the black depths of his eyes told Gabe that he had come to a favorable decision. "I'll tell you this," the old man said in a low voice. "Because of your background, I think you will understand. These other men, these men of Spanish blood, and those who say they have Spanish blood, although they actually have very little, they talk about the glory of the old days. But for the Indian, señor, the old days were not a glory at all. For the Indian, the coming of the Spaniard was a disaster from which he will never recover."

Gabe nodded. "I have seen something of that in my own land."

The old man went on as if Gabe had not spoken. "My father and my father's fathers had lived in this land since the beginning of time. This was their place, and in it, they lived a life that was like a happy dream. It was never cold, the sea teemed with fish, the land was rich with deer and rabbit. All had been put there for us. We collected the acorns that the trees dropped on the ground for our use. We pounded and cured their soft insides into a delicious flour. We had our own bread, señor, before the Spanish ever came!"

His eyes grew hooded. He looked down at the ground. "And then . . . the Spaniards. Those men of God, Father Serra, Crespi. They captured my people, herded them into their missions, made slaves of them. Slaves who were considered less than human."

He looked up, straight into Gabe's eyes again. "These men talk about horses. In the early days, Indians were forbidden to ride horses. If they were caught on the back of a horse, they were killed, señor. They were killed on the spot.

"And the missions. The endless days of labor, the nights locked in our rooms, the men apart from the women. And all the time, the land, our land, outside the barred windows, beckoning to us. But . . . if one of us managed to get away, they sent the soldiers after us, hunted us with dogs, and when we were brought back in chains, we were beaten as if we were animals. That is how those men of God treated my people."

He fell silent for a while, then spoke again. "My father was very good at getting away. The soldiers were very good at catching him. When the Spaniards got tired of that game, they killed him. The priests ordered the soldiers to beat my father to death, señor. In front of his own people, as a lesson. I say, a curse on those men of God. On Serra, on Crespi, on the rest of them. But," he said, laughing bitterly. "A curse is the White Man's way, is it not?"

Gabe looked at the old man, wondering. He was dressed like the rest, spoke like the rest, obviously, despite his bitterness, he made his home among them.

The old Indian saw the question in Gabe's eyes. "There is nothing left out there, señor," he said sadly. "It has all been destroyed. There is nothing left for me but this rancho. And perhaps that, too, will now be destroyed."

# CHAPTER NINE

It was when she slipped that he took her hand. He suspected that she had slipped on purpose. Even though the ground was rough, up until then she'd walked with the grace and sureness of a cat.

Not that he wanted to complain. Her hand was warm, and although strong from the work she did, smooth, nice to touch. He helped her balance as she jumped over a little fold in the ground, and as her hand automatically tightened in his, she looked up at him and smiled. With their hands joined, her face was fairly close. He found himself thinking that he'd never realized her skin looked so soft, so smooth. And those eyes. They were sparkling with happiness as she looked at him. And maybe with something more. Way too much more.

He let go of her hand reluctantly, aware that she withdrew it just as reluctantly. He suspected that if he reached out for her hand again, she would offer it gladly. Then they could walk hand in hand, a wonderful thought, but a treacherous one. This was Jorge's sister. Even if that were not the case, he wanted to do nothing that would be unfair to the girl. He was a wandering man. What if he took too much from her, played with her, then rode off some day, leaving her behind, ruined? He knew how the Spanish viewed the "honor" of their women. No, he must be careful not to compromise the girl. That he would never do to Mercedes.

"Your finger," she said, breaking into his thoughts, as if aware of their nature and wanting to banish them. "What happened to it?"

She was referring to the crooked index finger on his right hand, the hand she'd just been holding. Gabe shrugged. "An accident."

She shook her head. "No. Tell me."

"Well . . . a fight. When I was younger."

"Against an Indian?"

"No. A soldier."

"In a battle against the soldiers?"

She sounded both intrigued and a little horrified. He knew she was proud of her Indian blood, which was unusual among the Latins, who liked to pretend they were one hundred percent Spanish, even if their features proclaimed a more mixed heritage. But she had also grown up at war with the local Indians.

He shook his head. He had not wanted to get into this, but now he felt he had to clear it up. "No. At a fort. It actually started three years before the finger got broken. I was pitching hay into a corral one day, with a pitchfork, when—"

"But," she exclaimed, "I thought you lived with the Indians!"

"Only until I was fourteen. Then I went to live at the fort. My mother . . ."

His voice trailed away. Mercedes granted him a moment's silence, but her eyes begged him to continue. "When I was fourteen, my mother thought it would be better for me if I lived at the fort," he finally said. "Among the White Men, so that I could . . . learn about them. Learn about that part of me."

He did not say that his mother had urged an old friend, the Indian scout, Jim Bridger, to kidnap him one night from her lodge and take him to the fort by force. He still felt anger when he remembered the way he'd been tied up like a chicken and carted to the fort very much against his will. Bridger had told him it was his mother's idea, so that he would not try to go back. He had hated her for her betrayal, for banishing him to a place where the white people treated him like a dog, because he'd lived among Indians. Three years of slavery . . .

It was only much later that he understood why she had done it. For him. Being white herself, she had understood the overwhelming power of the whites, what terrible force they could bring to bear against the People. She had understood this in a way none of the Oglala, among whom she and her son lived, would ever be able to . . . until it was too late. She did not want her son dying a useless death fighting beside the Oglala against heavily armed soldiers, in a war that could have only one ending.

It had taken him a long time to forgive his mother; he regretted the six years he'd lost, away from the People. Three of those six years spent in the guardhouse. Because of the fight Mercedes wanted to hear about.

"I was seventeen at the time," he said. "The cavalry captain I mentioned, a man named Price, insulted me, tried to hit me. He was drunk. I hit him instead, and when he tried to draw his gun and shoot me, I stuck the pitchfork I was holding through his wrist."

Mercedes cocked her head to one side. "But . . . it sounds like you won the fight." She pointed to his hand. "Your finger . . ."

Gabe laughed bitterly. "Oh, I won the fight. But for winning it against a cavalry captain, me, a boy who'd lived with dirty savages, they locked me up. Put me in the guardhouse. For three years."

Mercedes looked at him somberly. "That must have been very difficult. For a man like you. For a man who loves his freedom."

"Don't all men?" he asked quickly. But yes, it had been hard. Locked away from the land, the sun, the sky. Those three years had seemed like thirty.

"How did you get out?" she asked.

"A friend. He talked to the colonel. Got me released."

He did not mention that the man who'd gotten him released had been the same man who'd kidnapped him and taken him to the fort. Jim Bridger. Supposedly, to work as a scout for the army. In reality, to warn the Oglala that a large force of soldiers would be coming through their land. Gabe was to persuade them to get out of the army's way, to move the villages to safety. He'd sure done a bad job of that. And it had cost him. Cost him terribly.

"But," Mercedes prompted, "you still haven't told me about the finger."

He looked over at her. They had stopped walking. She was leaning against a tree, her hands behind her back. Her position pulled her breasts high. Through the thin material of her blouse, he could see the points of her nipples. He tore his gaze away, glanced up at her eyes, and was sure he saw a momentary gleam there, a gleam of triumph that he'd bothered to notice.

Damn. She troubled him, all right. Not just her beauty, but her mind, too. With most girls, he would treat the questions she'd been asking as an annoyance, something to be disposed of curtly. But he knew she was not a brainless little flirt. She had a good mind; she was asking these questions to draw him out, to make him give her a little of his life. Because she was interested in him. Hell, she wanted him; he had no doubt of that. He wanted her, too. But . . .

"Ah, the finger," he finally said. "Well, after I got out of the guardhouse, this same captain set up a trap, with the help of some other officers. They cornered me in a barn. The captain had a pitchfork, and he was going to kill me with it, or at least hurt me very badly. When he came at me, I tried to grab the pitchfork, but one of the tines went through my hand. See," he said, holding his palm out toward her, showing her the puckered scar of an old puncture wound.

She took his hand, studied the scar, then looked up into his face. She didn't say anything stupid, like, "It must have hurt," just looked him in the eye, her own eyes full of understanding, and . . . a lot more?

"Well, we fought a while longer, after I got the pitchfork away from him, and then I hit him in the face. Broke his jaw, I hit him so hard. But because of the hole from the pitchfork, I couldn't close my fist tight enough, and the finger broke. Just the way you see it now."

She nodded. "You sound different when you talk about things like that. More . . . alive."

"Yes. It was a good fight." His eyes glowed as he remembered the scene in the barn, the hopelessness of his situation . . . until Jim Bridger had stepped out of the darkness, cocking his big Sharps carbine, the same carbine Gabe carried now, throwing down on the cowardly officers who would have been willing to watch Price kill him. Then, Bridger helping him get away after the fight. Helping him return to the Oglala, where he belonged, where he had found life again.

He tore his mind away from his memories. Pain lay there. Perhaps Mercedes sensed it; she stopped asking about his past, turned to the future. "I suppose you will ride away from here some day."

He nodded. "I suppose so."

She looked him straight in the eye. "I wish you wouldn't."

He started to reply, but shut his mouth. How could he say that it was because of her that he would ride away? Sooner than she thought. Because of wanting her, and knowing he could not have her. How could he say anything at all, while looking into those beautiful eyes, sensing the warmth and softness of her, so aware of her body, although several feet separated them?

Suddenly, a reprieve. Their attention was drawn away from one another as they heard the sound of galloping hooves approaching the ranch, followed by excited shouting. A look of sudden alarm appeared on Mercedes's face, just a fleeting moment of fright, quickly replaced by concern, curiosity. "We'd better . . ." she started to say, but Gabe had already taken her hand and was leading her back toward the ranch buildings, unaware that he even had her hand until they were nearly there. Then, feeling its soft heat and the vibrant weight of her body following, he suddenly became conscious of how naturally they'd touched, and he immediately let go.

They came out of the trees to find the ranch yard in an uproar. Two vaqueros were sitting lathered horses, talking excitedly, but from the smiles on their faces Gabe knew that it wasn't trouble. They were speaking so rapidly, and amidst such a hubbub from a rapidly gathering crowd of onlookers, that Gabe could not make out what they were saying. "What is it?" he asked Mercedes, whose eyes were shining with excitement.

"A bear," she said, turning toward him. "They've found a bear. They're going after it, but they need help."

"My rifle. I'll get it," Gabe said, turning toward the house.

To his surprise, Mercedes shook her head. "No. You won't need a rifle. Just your reata."

Gabe was puzzled. How the hell could you kill a bear with a reata? But, as he'd read in one of his grandfather's books . . . When in Rome . . .

So he jumped aboard one of the horses standing ready and saddled near the house, one of the *caballos del día*, horses of the day. Other men were doing the same. Within minutes a dozen men were mounted and ready to ride. Gabe spent a moment getting the animal under control; it was not as accustomed to him as his big black, but he never rode the black for any of the ranch work. It was trained for war, not as a cow pony.

The two men who'd found the bear had the honor of leading the others out of the ranch yard. As his horse started after the others, Gabe turned in the saddle, looking back for a moment. Mercedes was standing in the middle of the yard, looking after him. "Be careful," he heard her call out, and he knew it was to him she was calling.

As he looked back at her, young, beautiful, with her dark hair pulled behind her head, he felt a terrible wrenching pang inside himself, as he remembered how the Oglala women had called after their men as they rode out to the hunt or to war. His heart nearly broke with the weight of memory.

# CHAPTER TEN

The bear had been spotted about five miles away, where the valley gave way to rugged mountain slopes. A man had been left behind, to keep track of the animal. As they drew near the area, Gabe saw the man, sitting his horse on a hillside, vigorously waving his poncho to gain the attention of the approaching riders.

There were seven of them including Gabe and Jorge. The *capataz* flashed Gabe a big grin. "Now, my friend," he said, "you will see something you will never forget."

Gabe shrugged. If Jorge meant the bear, there it was, about three hundred yards away, a big silvertip grizzly, and he'd seen plenty of grizzlies. The bear, which had been ambling along, saw the riders approaching. It had no doubt been aware of the lookout left behind and had tolerated him, but with another seven men coming straight at it, the bear decided that it would be best to leave for other parts.

Gabe watched the bear shuffle along. It had already built up a big reserve of fat for the approaching winter; its massive sides shook and shuddered with each step. It looked slow and clumsy, but that was deceptive; that shambling trot was eating up distance. The men had to urge their horses into a lope to keep up. Not that the horses were all that eager to get closer to the bear. Somewhere in their dim, little, ruminant minds,

horses understood that bears had been eating their kind for
aeons.

But they were well-trained, or maybe more afraid of
their riders than of the bear, and the little group of horsemen quickly gained on the retreating grizzly.

"Look!" Jorge said excitedly. "He's heading for a cave."

Sure enough, Gabe could see the dark mouth of a cave set
in a rock cliff a few hundred yards ahead. Probably the bear's
winter resting place. "We have to head him off before he can
hide in there," Jorge said. "Come on!"

Three riders raced away with Jorge. After a moment's
hesitation, Gabe followed. He was not at all sure what the
men intended to do. Not one of them had brought a rifle.
A couple of the riders other than himself had pistols, but a
revolver was next to useless against a bear as big as the one
they were chasing.

Following Jorge's lead, they rode around in front of the
bear, cutting it off from sanctuary in the cave. The grizzly,
beginning to grow annoyed now, stood up on his hind legs
for a moment, glaring at the men in front of him. Gabe could
hear his angry growl.

Gabe still had no idea what was supposed to happen.
Would they simply tease the bear for a while, then ride
away? That might not be smart. A grizzly, charging over
short distances, could run faster than a horse could turn and
start away.

Then Gabe saw several of the men shaking out their
reatas, their lassos, and he began to get a glimmering
of the plan. At the ranch, he'd seen the way the men
used the reatas; they were masters with a loop. Since
he'd decided to stay at the ranch, he'd carried a reata
at his own saddle horn. Not that he could use it the way
the vaqueros did. His reata was made of six strands of
rawhide carefully braided together to form a thin rope of
amazing strength and flexibility. His was only about sixty
feet long, but he'd seen some of over a hundred feet. He'd
also seen vaqueros dab a noose over a running cow's head
at sixty feet.

The bear was down on all fours again, this time heading

off to one side, trying to slip away from the riders, who had now almost encircled him. Gabe saw the first loop thrown, from about forty feet. It caught the bear by the left front leg. The bear jerked its leg backward, trying to shake off the loop, but the rider snubbed it around his saddle horn and backed his horse away.

Uh-oh, Gabe thought. That rider's in a lot of trouble. By now the bear was very much aware of where this latest problem was coming from. Gabe could see the big grizzly's muscles bunch as it got ready to rush the man who'd roped him.

But before it could start moving, another reata snaked out. This time the loop settled around the bear's right hind leg. The bear had just started to move, but when the reata tightened on its hind leg, it fell flat on its face.

The bear did not stay down for more than a couple of seconds. Springing back up onto its feet, the bear let out an awesome roar of rage. Gabe could feel his horse trembling, but, well-trained, it did not try to run.

The bear began to tug at the ropes binding its two legs. Gabe could see the horses to which the reatas were attached begin to lose their balance.

Then another rawhide rope hissed through the air. This one settled around the bear's massive throat. The grizzly managed to stand on its hind legs, pawing at the thin rawhide loop that was choking it, until the two reatas attached to its legs were tightened again, and the bear fell a second time.

More reatas were thrown, one more around the bear's neck, and one each around its two remaining free legs. The loops were tightened. The bear was splayed out on the ground helpless. Gabe could hear the bear gasping for breath as the nooses around its neck cut off its air. Well, that was it, then. The vaqueros were going to choke it to death. A messy way for the bear to die. Gabe would have preferred a quick shot to the heart, with the struggle over cleanly.

Jorge read his expression. "Sometimes we do choke them to death," he said. "But not this time. We want this bear alive."

"Alive?" Gabe asked in wonder. "You intend to capture a full-grown grizzly, alive?"

Jorge nodded vigorously. "It's time for a little sport. The bull and the bear. We will have a big fiesta, and Señor *Oso*, there," he said, pointing to the wheezing bear, "will be our guest of honor."

A bull baiting. Gabe had seen it before, did not particularly like it. But the rest of the men were obviously looking forward to it. Why else would they risk their necks, capturing such a dangerous animal? But how the hell were they going to get it back to the ranch? He saw no cage. Maybe one was on the way. Would they choke the bear unconscious, then shove it into the cage? He sure as hell had no intention of getting close enough to manhandle a live grizzly.

But there was no cage on the way. Instead, the vaqueros led the bear, very unwillingly, right back to the ranch. They let the bear get its breath back, then loosened some of the ropes, giving the bear the impression that, even if it didn't get away, it just might have a chance to make mincemeat out of one of its tormentors. So, as soon as the ropes slackened, it charged the nearest horse and rider.

It was a horse and rider who lay in the direction of the ranch. The bear was allowed to charge a few yards, then the ropes tightened, and down it went. This maneuver was repeated again and again. Twice more they had to choke the bear, when its furious struggles threatened to pull horses off balance. Occasionally, they were able to lead the grizzly along like a huge dog on a set of very long leashes.

It took all day to get the bear back to the ranch. As they approached, Gabe could see people pouring out of the buildings, cheering at the sight of their unwilling guest's arrival. Faced by all the people and noise, the bear began to struggle harder than ever. Gabe, who up until now had been too impressed by the vaqueros' exhibition of riding skill to think of the bear, now began to feel sorry for the animal. It had looked so magnificent, shambling along free. Now, it had been made to look almost foolish. And would soon be a prisoner. While the riders had been away, others had been busy at the ranch. A big wooden cage had been constructed. It sat on open ground about a hundred yards from the main house.

Gabe had had his share of prison; he did not like to see anything locked up. But . . . it wouldn't be for long. The weekend was coming up, the day of the Christian god. The day when the Spaniards liked to have their fiestas. Liked to shed blood. That's when they would have the bull baiting.

The riders were having trouble coaxing the bear toward the cage; it was struggling fiercely, as if it understood that this was its final chance to get away. People were crowding in close, shouting, hoping that the noise would help force the grizzly into the cage. Gabe saw Mercedes, banging on a pan, her eyes sparkling with excitement. She was standing awfully close to the grizzly.

The bear made one last attempt to break away. Rearing up on its hind legs, it tore one reata loose from a saddle horn. The grizzly, its little eyes red with rage, was partially free. Gabe saw it start forward . . . straight toward Mercedes.

Without thinking, he rammed his heels into his horse's ribs, forcing the startled animal straight toward the bear. His reata was in his right hand, a loop trailing. He lashed out, whipping the reata across the bear's eyes and muzzle. For just a second, the bear, its eyes stinging from the impact of the rawhide, stopped to paw at its face. Another loop immediately settled around its neck and was pulled tight, but not before the bear took a final swipe at Gabe. He saw the grizzly's enormous claws slashing at him. He tried to back his horse away, but not quite quickly enough. The claws raked along his ribs, cutting through cloth and skin, not deeply, but almost immediately blood began to well up from the parallel rows of cuts.

It was the bear's last act of defiance. Choking, it was guided into the cage. The heavy wooden gate slammed shut. The bear was a prisoner.

Gabe's horse, wild-eyed with fright after such a close encounter with its ancient ursine enemy, was prancing wildly. Gabe had his hands full getting the terrified animal back under control. As the horse steadied, Gabe became aware that someone was standing next to him; there was a hand on his leg. He looked down. The hand belonged to Mercedes. Her eyes were big, frightened.

"You're hurt," she called up to him.

"It's nothing," he replied. But his side really did hurt, not that he'd ever let it show. That had been the primary lesson of his youth . . . never to show pain, not even if you'd just had your guts blown out.

"But it is something," the girl insisted. "A bear's claws are very dirty. You could get an infection. Get down from the horse. We will have to clean those cuts."

He swung down, more annoyed then worried. The bear had ruined one of his favorite shirts. Hell, one of his only shirts. A vaquero led his horse away, while Mercedes quite firmly guided Gabe toward the house where she lived with Jorge and his family. "I have alcohol inside," she said. "And cloth to wrap up the cuts."

He wanted to tell her it was all a lot of trouble for nothing, but he knew she was right. He'd seen men die from terrible infections, via the claws of animals. Besides, what a fine excuse to walk along beside Mercedes.

Mercedes led the way inside. He'd expected the house to be crowded as usual, full of children, women, and activity, but it was empty. Everyone was outside, looking at the bear.

He stood alone, looking about the crowded living room of Jorge's house, while Mercedes rummaged through shelves, collecting alcohol, old cloth, and a battered tin of what looked like salve. When she had what she needed, she came over to him, and without any preliminaries, began unbuttoning his shirt. He wanted to tell her that he could do it himself, but decided to keep his mouth shut. Partly because he liked it this way. He was intensely aware of the girl's closeness, of the heat of her body, the sweet female odor that emanated from her flesh.

She stripped away the bloody shirt, then peered closely at the three long cuts on the right side of his torso. He did not deign to pay attention to such minor wounds.

"The cuts are not very deep," she said. "But I will clean them. Sit down."

She guided him backward, to a chair. When the chair's

seat hit the back of his knees, he had little choice but to sit. He was surprised when Mercedes knelt on the floor in front of him; he'd expected her to stand. She crowded right in between his legs. Very close.

She'd brought a pan of water and began to sponge his wounded ribs with a wet cloth. The cuts stung a little. Then they stung a lot when she wet another cloth with alcohol and scrubbed the alcohol into the cuts. Gabe concentrated on keeping his face immobile. Mercedes smiled up at him, perhaps a little mockingly. "Ah, what magnificent machismo," she said drily. "As impressive as any *Californio's*."

The alcohol evaporated quickly, and while it dried, she tore pieces of cloth into long strips. But before wrapping the cuts, she applied some of the salve. It smelled terrible. "I think you saved me from getting very badly hurt," Mercedes said. "The bear . . ."

Gabe shrugged. Then he had an image of the bear reaching Mercedes, its huge claws ripping her beautiful face to shreds. He shuddered.

"Oh, did I hurt you?" she asked in alarm.

"No. It was something else."

By now she was wrapping the cloth around his body. She leaned in close, concentrating. He was enormously aware that her breasts was pressing against him. He tried not to become aroused. He'd make himself forget about her breasts. While she continued her work, he looked down at her. How beautiful her face was, seen this close. How lovely her hair.

She finished wrapping the wound, tying off the cloth. "There," she said. "More scars to go with the ones you already have."

She was studying his naked torso above the bandage. Before he knew what he was going to do, she began running her fingers over the network of old scars that crisscrossed his chest and arms. Her fingertips felt like hot pokers searing his flesh. "I guess you don't bother to get out of the way when something comes flying in your direction," she said. "You should take better care of yourself. I would not like anything to happen to you."

She looked up him, while her right hand still lay against his chest. Looking down into her huge brown eyes, he felt something inside him let loose, something that gave way, leaving him defenseless. He was drowning in her eyes; his body throbbed at her touch. He had an overwhelming urge to reach out, touch her face, touch that soft skin, draw her close to him. She seemed to be waiting for him to do just that. Somewhat impatiently.

"I," he muttered, starting to stand up. "Mercedes . . . I . . . Jorge. He's your brother . . . my friend. I wouldn't like to . . ."

She stayed on her knees for a moment, still looking up at him, her face still soft. Then anger began to change those lovely contours. She stood up quickly, shook out her skirts, then spun around and headed for the door. She stopped just short of the door, and turned to face him. "You idiot!" she snapped. "Don't you know that Jorge would be delighted?"

Then she was gone, leaving Gabe standing in the middle of the room, naked to the waist, bandaged, and feeling, indeed, very much like an idiot.

# CHAPTER ELEVEN

Gabe spent a miserable night with little sleep, most of it broken by way too much thinking. Confused thinking. What had Mercedes meant about Jorge? What would delight him? The dishonoring of his sister?

Gabe got up the next morning in as bad a mood as the grizzly they'd caught the day before. After a breakfast he barely tasted, he wandered over to the bear's cage. Why he was there, he didn't know. Maybe just to see another confused male.

Several children had gathered. Standing well back from the cage, most were obviously awestruck as they stared in through the wooden bars at the huge bear. One boy, more daring than the rest, grinning evilly, picked up a stick, ran close to the cage, and poked the stick through the bars, right into the bear's silver-tipped flank. The bear roared and charged the bars, smashing at them with his enormous paws. The cage shook and creaked, and for a moment Gabe thought it might break.

He grabbed the boy by the arm. "Don't do that again," he said in a cold voice. "Unless you have the courage to do it when the bear is loose and has a chance to fight back. Only then will your act have any meaning."

The boy slunk away; by now the other children had scattered, screaming in fear. Gabe turned to face the bear.

It had quieted by now and stood facing Gabe. Its eyes, seeming small in that massive head, met his. They both looked solemnly at one another for a few seconds. It was Gabe who looked away first; he did not like the fate that awaited the animal. He quickly walked away.

Later that day, while he was helping some of the men saddle-break new horses, Mercedes came from one of the kitchens, bringing water for the vaqueros. As always, when he saw her approaching, his pulse quickened. He watched her walk all the way across the yard, watched the swing of her legs beneath her skirt, watched the way her long black hair blew out behind her in the breeze. He was particularly aware of the dark beauty of her eyes.

But those eyes avoided him, looked everywhere but where he was standing. He watched her when she left, a little relieved that he didn't have to talk to her. Not after that scene in the house the day before. He'd made such a mess of it. But, as she walked away, he felt a sense of loss. In general, he felt terrible.

He saw her from time to time over the next couple of days, usually from a distance. The time or two when they were in each other's company, each made it a point not to talk to the other. Of course, other people were becoming aware of this byplay. Once, Gabe caught a glimpse of a puzzled look on Jorge's face.

Still, Gabe reasoned, it was best this way. A slow cooling of a situation that had grown too hot, too dangerous, especially in this tight little community. Nothing could be hidden here. In time, things would return to normal, and he and Mercedes could be civil to one another again. If he had not left the ranch by then. The days were piling up, one after the other, each day pretty much like the day that had preceded it. Life at El Rancho de Las Palomas was unchanging, a steady routine. Time, flying away. There was still so much world to see and so little time. He was aware of the danger that he might lose his sense of wonder about the world, along with the desire to see it. Each day he spent at the ranch immersed him a little deeper into its way of life. For the first time in quite a while he was beginning to feel that he belonged somewhere. Dangerous, because it was an illusion. He did not really belong at all.

Sunday finally arrived, the day chosen for the bull and bear baiting. One of the larger corrals had been built up higher and stronger. Seats had been constructed of planks and logs, just outside the corral, so that people could watch in comfort. The bear had been let out of its cage during the very early morning. That had been a tricky operation. A chain had been passed around its left rear leg, with the other end made fast to a big post imbedded in the center of the corral. When the bear finally came boiling out of the cage, he made straight for the nearest vaquero, who ran as if the devil himself were on his tail. The chain tightened, and the bear fell, sprawling.

They gave the bear most of the morning to grow used to the chain, to what its limits were. As the bear paced around and around the post, the fiesta began. Meat was being cooked, wine and beer were flowing, a festive mood filled the air.

By a little past midday, most of the populace of El Rancho de Las Palomas was seated in the stands overlooking the corral, which was about to become an arena. Gabe took a seat off to one side, a little apart from the others. He could see Mercedes, seated on the far side. Don Andres had the seat of honor, right in the center.

The bear, upset by the crowd, was pacing even more nervously. From time to time he rose on his hind legs, to rake the pole with his claws. His eyes were glittering madly. Someone in the crowd began to throw stones at the bear, and soon many were doing the same. It was not random cruelty, but rather a calculated move to anger the big grizzly, to make it want to fight.

Now the fight was about to begin. A chute was opened on the far side of the corral. Reatas cracked against hide, and a moment later an enormous longhorn bull came trotting into the corral, obviously mad as hell.

A cheer went up from the crowd. The bull, alarmed by the noise, tossed its horns angrily.

Then the bull saw the bear. The bull stopped dead in its tracks, its eyes focused on the grizzly.

The grizzly had already seen the bull. It now had a focus for the rage that had been gnawing at it for the past few days. Standing to its full height on its rear legs, it let out a mighty roar, its forepaws clawing at the air.

The bull took up the challenge. Bellowing angrily, it pawed the ground, shaking its horns from side to side. Gabe figured that the spread of the horns was more than six feet across.

A well-thrown stone, thumping into the bull's hind-quarters, galvanized it into action. Spraying dirt and bellowing, it charged straight toward the bear.

The bear showed its nimbleness by partially sidestepping the bull. One of the bull's horns barely missed the bear's side. As the bull rushed past, the grizzly's claws raked bloody furrows along its flank.

Bellowing in pain and anger, the bull spun around and charged again. This time the two huge animals collided head on. The bear was fortunate in the width of the bull's horns; their sharp points thrust past the sides of his body, but the central boss was pressed into the bear's belly, and the bull, pawing for purchase, began to drive the bear backward.

With a mighty swing of its paws, the bear twisted the bull's horns, sending the bull spinning away, onto its side. Roaring in triumph, the bear rushed the fallen bull, ready to finish it off . . . until all the slack in its chain had been used up and the bear was jolted to a sudden halt, a yard short of the bull.

The bull rolled to its feet, then backed away several yards. Snorting, pawing the dirt, it eyed its adversary with new respect. But the rage flooding through its tiny brain won out over fear, and it charged again.

The bear made the mistake of waiting for the bull at the limit of its chain, which restricted its movements. Once again the bull collided with the bear, but this time the bear was unable to move to the side. One of the bull's horns pierced its abdomen.

The crowd screamed in delight. The bear, bellowing in pain, tried to back away from the horn impaling it, but the bull kept pressing forward, trying to grind the horn in deeper. Finally, the bear raised one massive paw, and with desperate strength, smashed the paw down against the bull's neck, breaking its spine.

The bull dropped in its tracks, as suddenly as the steer on which old Miguel had performed the *nuqueo* at the last fiesta. As it went down, its horn slipped out of the bear's body, shiny with blood. The bear backed away, pressing its paws to the wound the way a man might do with his hand. It began to moan, a pitiful sound, but the crowd loved it.

Gabe nodded his head once toward the bear. A brave animal, it had fought well. Now would be a good time to shoot it, before the pain grew any greater. It had earned a quick death.

But to Gabe's surprise the chute opened again and another bull was chased into the arena. This new bull had not only the loud cheering to make it nervous, and the smell of the bear, but also the smell of blood and death.

The bull trotted all the way around the arena, avoiding the dead bull, watching the bear out of one eye, measuring, wondering if there might not be some way it could get out of this. But there was no way; stones pelted its back, maddening an already nervous animal. There was nothing on which it could take out its rage except the wounded bear.

The crowd screamed with joy as the bull charged. The two animals came together with a sodden thud and stood struggling.

Gabe was beginning to grow angry. The bear's valor had gone unappreciated. All that the crowd wanted was blood and entertainment. Disgusted, Gabe slipped out of his seat and walked away behind the stands.

He was surprised when he turned and saw Mercedes, standing about thirty feet away, angrily kicking at a clod of dirt. She looked up and saw him. For the first time in days, something approaching communication passed between them.

Gabe walked over to Mercedes and her clod of dirt. "You look angry," he said.

"I am," she snapped back. "I've never liked these things. They're so . . . without honor."

Gabe nodded. "I feel the same way."

She looked up, surprised. "You? But I thought, well . . . that the Indians . . ."

"Liked torture?" He was smiling wryly. "Sometimes it happened, usually to a tribal enemy. His torture was a way of seeing how brave he was. Cowards were killed on the spot. I later grew to dislike that kind of thing very much."

Gabe's mind was filled with ugly images of himself castrating and slashing a wounded soldier, a man he had once seen beat an old Indian with a rifle butt. He had not felt clean for days afterward. He had never again done anything like that.

There was another scream from the crowd. He and Mercedes turned toward the sound, heard the bear howl in pain, heard the bull bellowing wildly.

Mercedes turned away sharply. "I don't want to stay here," she said in a low voice. "Please . . . keep me company."

Walking about five feet apart, they wandered slowly away from the corral, toward the back of the main house. For a while, neither said anything. It was Mercedes who finally broke the silence. "When I was treating your cuts the other day, I saw some strange scars on your arms and chest. Long thin scars. I've been trying to figure out what might have made them."

She briefly glanced over at him, her face grave. "Was it torture?"

He gave a small, almost bitter laugh. "Torture? Yes, I suppose. Self-inflicted, to do something about the torture inside. Those are mourning scars which I gave myself, with my own knife, the day I buried my mother and my wife. After they were killed."

Mercedes looked stricken. "Wife? I didn't know you had a wife. My God! Who killed them?"

"A soldier," Gabe said bleakly. "Shot my wife in the head. She'd already been shot in the stomach. Then the same man ran my mother through with a saber."

Instinctively, Mercedes took a step toward him, laid a comforting hand on his arm. "I'm sorry I asked."

"No . . . you couldn't have known, and sometimes I have to think about it."

But he did not like to think about it. He remembered the soldiers pouring into the sleeping village, the thunder of horses' hooves, the screaming of the wounded and dying, the smell of blood. Like the smell of blood back in the corral, but that time it had not been a bear's blood. Human blood. And some of it had been the blood of his mother and his wife.

He told her a little about it. He also told her how, after he'd buried his mother and laid his wife on a burial platform in the Oglala style, he'd used his knife to make those cuts on his arms and chest, while he had howled out his grief. He did not tell her how, after the battle, he'd had to kill his stepfather, who, maddened by his own grief, had tried to kill Gabe simply because Gabe had white skin, like the soldiers.

"How could soldiers do that, kill two women?" Mercedes asked, shaking her head in wonderment.

"Easily," Gabe replied flatly. "That day they killed a lot of women. And old men, and children, even babies. And not only that day. Besides, the man who slaughtered my family had a personal reason."

Mercedes looked at him, confused. Gabe held up his right hand, showing her the broken finger, the puncture wound. "It was the same man who did this. The cavalry captain I told you about. I had beaten him in two fights. He wanted revenge. What better revenge than to kill my wife and my mother?"

Gabe remembered it all so vividly. Yellow Buckskin Girl's head snapping back as the bullet went in near her eye. The saber disappearing into his mother's chest. All while Gabe watched and could do nothing, because he had a baby under each arm, trying to save them from the soldiers.

Finally Mercedes spoke again. "And this man, this cavalry captain . . ."

"He died," Gabe said in an expressionless voice, as he stared straight ahead. "Not that day. It took me a while to find him."

They walked a few more steps. "He died hard," Gabe added in a low voice. He was unaware of Mercedes recoiling slightly from the look on his face. Gabe was remembering the burning barn, the white snow, and Captain Stanley Price running from that barn, a living ball of fire, screaming in agony, finally falling onto the snow, which melted around him as he died. He deserved no mercy. A fighter of boys. A killer of women and children.

Tracking down Stanley Price had changed his life. Following the captain, he'd met his grandfather in Boston. The old man had spent a lot of time introducing Gabe to the White Man's ways, opening his eyes to new worlds. He'd had a white friend, too. Rory. He would like to see Rory again. Would like to see a lot of people again. But too many of them were dead.

After Price's death, he'd returned to the Oglala. Fought alongside Red Cloud against the soldiers. But then he had left the People, not willing to see their final degradation, which he knew would eventually come at the hands of the whites.

"I'm glad he's dead, that captain," Mercedes said quietly. "It would not be right for a man like that to survive."

They were nearing the stand of trees behind the house. Mercedes spoke again. "I told you what I don't like about the bear and the bull, because of the way they are made to fight. Without honor, for the amusement of others. But there is more. When they brought the bear here and locked it up, I thought of you, something strong, brought down by puny, less noble creatures. I love my people, but when they do these things, I become angry with them."

"They're only human. And we humans . . ."

He stopped speaking. What had he been about to say? That humans do crazy things? Perhaps crazy like the way he felt about this girl.

They walked in among the trees. Finally, Gabe had to ask. "What did you mean the other day—that Jorge would be delighted?"

She stopped walking and turned to face him. "Just what you think," she replied. "What you already know. That my brother thinks very highly of you. It would make him happy if we . . . if there were another tie binding you here."

Gabe stepped back. "And it doesn't bother you that your own brother would use you . . . ?"

She shook her head in wonderment. "Use me? Are you blind, Gabe? How could Jorge be using me, when he knows that. . . . it's what I want, too."

They were standing about a yard apart. Mercedes looked down at the ground, a little abashed by her declaration. Gabe studied her, from her glistening black hair to the small feet peeping from beneath her skirt. His mind was racing. So many places to see, so little time. He remembered the pain he had felt when Yellow Buckskin Girl had been killed. Since then, he had hesitated to become strongly attached to anyone else. Yet, the reality of this beautiful woman, standing so close, was weakening his resolve. Also, there was the reality of life at El Rancho de Las Palomas, that sense of belonging.

They slowly, almost hesitantly, came together. Mercedes raised her face as Gabe bent to kiss her. It was a gentle kiss at first, growing more heated as their arms tightened around one another. Gabe was aware of Mercedes's breasts pressing against his chest, of the long line of her legs beneath the skirt, and of her increasingly rapid breathing, the way she strained against him. He heard her give a little moan, and he had no doubt it was fueled by desire.

Hard to tell what might have happened between them, screened from the rest of the ranch by the trees, if an uproar had not suddenly broken out near the corral, an uproar quite different from the roar of the mob as they watched two animals kill one another. First, there was a wild pounding of hooves, followed by individual shouts. Shouts of alarm. They could hear people running.

Gabe and Mercedes broke apart. Gabe looked into Mercedes's flushed features, imagined his own looked just as flushed.

"Help him down from the horse!" they heard someone shout.

Another look between Gabe and Mercedes, and then they were running toward the corral. They could see, even before they had arrived, that everyone had left their seats and were clustered around something on the ground. A riderless horse, lathered from a hard run, stood a few yards away. A quick look told Gabe there was blood on the saddle.

He and Mercedes pushed their way through the crowd. One of the vaqueros lay on the ground. Blood soaked his shirt and vest. Gabe recognized him as one of the men who had missed the fiesta; he'd been detailed to watch the herd. Gabe remembered his name as Pedro.

Don Andres was bent over Pedro, speaking to him. When the old man finally straightened up, his face was tight with anger.

"What is it?" someone called out.

"Banditos!" Don Andres snapped. "Those scum from Sonora are stealing our cattle." His eyes swept over the crowd. "To your horses, vaqueros. We must stop them!"

# CHAPTER TWELVE

Within a quarter of an hour, fourteen men were ready to ride, including Don Andres, Jorge, and Gabe. Mounting, they milled about the ranch yard for another half minute, checking their gear. Those left behind, mostly old men, women, and children, called out brave words to the departing warriors, but there was no masking the concern and fear in their eyes. Fear that some of those riding out would not ride back. The Sonora bandits had a reputation for brutal ferocity.

Mercedes stood among the crowd of women. She ran up to Jorge. He leaned down from his horse, kissed her on the cheek. Then she turned toward Gabe. Their eyes met. He was tempted to ride over and say good-bye, but Don Andres was already riding out of the yard, the men streaming along after him. Gabe and Mercedes's eyes met. The glance they shared said all that needed to be said.

The wounded Pedro had told them where he'd had his encounter with the bandits. Don Andres led the men straight in that direction. They were all feeling high-spirited, although Gabe doubted that many of them were fighters by nature, but rather, working men. What worried him was their armament. Few had modern weapons. He counted six men with muzzle-loading rifles, one with an old smooth-bore musket. Don Andres, Jorge, and two other men carried Winchesters. Most of the rest carried revolvers, although some of the guns were so old they looked like they might not function.

Nor was Gabe happy with the way Don Andres was riding straight ahead, without sending out scouts. Within half an hour they'd found the place where Pedro had been wounded. The ground was quite disturbed, but it was easy to see that ten or twelve men had driven away perhaps a hundred head of cattle. The trail was broad and straight, leading toward a pass several miles away.

Once again, Don Andres waved the men straight on. Gabe rode near the head of the little column, next to Jorge and Don Andres. He was carefully studying the terrain ahead. Finally, he laid his hand on Don Andres's arm. "Señor," he said, "if we could stop for just a moment . . ."

The old man was slightly annoyed, but his innate courtesy led him to grant Gabe his request. Gabe immediately dismounted, and, taking his binoculars, climbed to the top of a small rise, where he lay on his belly, carefully scanning the trail ahead.

When he came down from the rise, Don Andres was visibly fidgeting in his saddle. "They are getting away," the old man grumbled.

Jorge noticed the look on Gabe's face. "What did you see?" he asked.

"A fine place for an ambush. About a mile ahead."

"Ambush?" Don Andres said tartly. "They would not take the time. They will be pushing straight for the border. With my cattle, by God! And if we hesitate any longer . . ."

Gabe shrugged. "Perhaps. But if there is an ambush, and they force us to stop for a long time to take care of our dead and wounded, they will make it to the border all the more easily."

"What do you suggest?" Jorge cut in.

Gabe pointed off to one side. "That I take four men with me, then loop around to the right. See that high point over there? It overlooks the place where a clever man might set an ambush. We can reach it in ten minutes. If there is no ambush, I will signal, and you can ride forward as fast as you want."

Jorge looked over at Don Andres. "What about it, *Patrón*?" the *capataz* asked. "If there is an ambush . . ."

The old man sat and fumed, but then he remembered the way Gabe had fought with him against the hired gunmen in Los Angeles. "All right," he grumbled. He turned to Gabe. "But ride fast. I don't want those *cabrónes* to get away with my cattle."

Gabe nodded, then quickly picked four men, choosing those with long-barreled, single-shot rifles that looked like they might be accurate at a good distance. Within a minute they had started to ride in a shallow loop around to the right of the main trail. Gabe had already noticed, from his vantage point on top of the rise, that gullies and streambeds would shield them from view most of the way.

They reached high ground in a little less than ten minutes. Gabe stopped behind a small ridge. Dismounting, he took his binoculars and went to the edge of the ridge alone.

He'd been right; there was an ambush. Six bandits had been left behind. They were hidden in a small gully, which masked their presence from the main trail, but their backs were badly exposed to the ridge on which Gabe was now lying. He carefully studied the men below. Swinging his glasses further to the right, he caught sight of the stolen herd, about half a mile away, moving slowly along a plateau. Several men were riding herd on the cattle, but they were too far away for Gabe to make out any details.

Gabe slipped back down the back side of the ridge. He issued quick, quiet orders. The horses were left behind, securely tied to small trees. Then he led his four men to the top of the ridge.

Once again, he studied the ambushers below. They were all heavily armed. He could see crossed ammunition belts, lever action rifles, and lots of pistols. The faces of the men were hidden beneath huge sombreros. Their horses had been tied about fifty yards behind them.

Gabe had brought his Sharps with him. He checked the cap; it looked good. But, before taking aim, he took time for one more piece of his strategy. He'd noticed that the bandits had looked nervous. They'd probably spotted Don Andres's men when they rode over a distant ridge, before disappearing into the gully where Gabe had left them. The bandits were probably wondering why their pursuers had not reappeared.

Gabe stood up on the ridge top, out of sight of the bandits, but not out of sight of Don Andres and the others. He waved. There was an answering wave, and the nine men with Don Andres started forward again.

Gabe lay down on the ridge top and picked up the Sharps. He estimated the range from the ridge to the bandits at a little over three hundred yards. He raised the Sharps's rear sight and set the crossbar for the correct range.

By now, the bandits had spotted Don Andres and his men. Gabe saw the bandits shift into firing position. Another few minutes, and the vaqueros would be within rifle range.

Gabe spread his own four men out on the ridge top. He told them not to fire until he had fired. Then he lay on his belly and settled down to aim, centering his sights on one of the bandits.

He'd already pulled the set trigger. Now the main trigger would release at very light pressure. He began to exert that pressure, very slowly, while holding his breath, so that nothing would disturb the lay of his rifle. A little more pressure . . .

The Sharps seemed to go off by itself, slamming Gabe's shoulder back. Peering through a dense cloud of white smoke, Gabe saw one of the bandits fly about a foot off the ground as the Sharps's huge seven hundred grain bullet slammed into his body.

The four men with Gabe now opened fire, too. Most of their shots were misses; it was long range for their antique weapons, but Gabe saw one bandit thrown sideways. Gabe reloaded as quickly as he could. Within twenty seconds, he was firing again. His second shot hit another bandit.

By now, the bandits who'd been left behind in ambush were firing back up at the ridge, but their Winchesters did not have enough range. And the firing pinpointed their position to Don Andres. Gabe saw the old man rise up in the saddle, wave his right hand, and lead his whooping warriors straight toward the little gully.

The three surviving bandits tried to break and run; to stay in the gully was to be picked off one by one by the riflemen behind them, up on the ridge. Don Andres's group swept down on the fleeing bandits. Gabe watched two go down with pistol balls in their bodies. He also saw Don Andres lean down out of his saddle. Swinging the short sword he carried under his left leg, Don Andres split the last man's skull.

Gabe stood up. "Make sure you reload," he told his men. When he was certain that each man was carrying at least one loaded weapon, he led the way down the back side of the ridge, to the horses.

"What do we do now?" one of the vaqueros asked, as he mounted.

"Go after the herd," Gabe replied tersely.

Which was what Don Andres was already doing. With the last of the ambushers taken care of, he was leading his vaqueros straight toward the mesa where the dust from his stolen herd could be seen. Gabe knew that Don Andres would get there first; he had the shortest way to go. Gabe's party would have to take a longer way around, but they'd hit the remaining bandits from the side.

Which was just the way it happened. Don Andres and his vaqueros had already reached the remaining bandits by the time Gabe came into view. Seeing how few men Don Andres had with him, and how poorly they were armed, the bandits had decided to stay and fight for the cattle they had stolen.

It was a bad mistake. While the bandits were pinned down by their fight with Don Andres and his men, Gabe and the four men with him plowed into their flank. Gabe had put the reloaded Sharps away and was now depending on the firepower of his Winchester. Levering rapidly, he used four shots to blow two bandits out of their saddles. He heard the old muskets of his men bellow once apiece, and then they were in among the bandits, blasting away with their revolvers.

Riding hard at the bandits, Gabe had an impression of

fierce men with huge drooping moustaches and enormous wide-brimmed hats. Each bandit was so heavily armed that Gabe wondered how their horses could take the weight. Each man had crossed ammunition belts for their Winchesters and as many as three pistols. The armament did them little good. Attacked from two sides, the bandits—there were six of them with the herd—were quickly shot down.

Stuffing more shells into his Winchester, Gabe noticed that Don Andres was pressing his horse toward a fallen bandit. Apparently, the man had been wounded only in the arm. Gabe saw Don Andres raise his pistol to finish off the bandit. The old man's face was twisted with battle lust.

"Wait!" Gabe called out.

The shout caused Don Andres to turn his head. He stared at Gabe uncomprehendingly.

"Let him live," Gabe said, riding close to the old ranchero.

"Let him live?" Don Andres demanded angrily. "After he and his companions have stolen my cattle, wounded some of my men? Why should I?"

Gabe stuffed his Winchester back into its saddle scabbard. "Look at him," he said, pointing to the bandit, who was cowering on the ground, holding his wounded arm. "He is no longer anyone to fear. Send him back to Sonora. Let him tell his bandit friends what happens to men who attack El Rancho de Las Palomas. Perhaps not very many will be willing to ride this way again."

Don Andres continued to look angry for a moment, then he suddenly began to laugh. "Of course," he said. "Send this dog to spread the news. Why not? We've killed enough of these scum today. By the beard of Christ, let the rest of that miserable pack hear how painful it is to attack our land."

The wounded bandit, hardly able to believe his luck, was placed on the sorriest of the bandits' horses, minus his arms and possessions. He hunched in his saddle, certain that it was a trick, that once he started to ride away, they would shoot him in the back. Just a little sport for the vaqueros. It was what he would have done if the tables had been turned.

A quirt end cracking across his horse's rump sent the animal lurching forward. The bandit nearly fell off the horse's back. The vaqueros watched him go, all of them laughing at the desperate way the bandit was holding onto the saddle horn.

Don Andres stood up in his stirrups and called after the disappearing bandit, "Go with the devil, *hijo de puta*! I doubt God would have you!"

# CHAPTER THIRTEEN

The victorious vaqueros rode into the ranch yard in a fierce, triumphant mood. Those who had waited behind came running to meet them. Their faces were drawn and anxious at first, until a quick, tense count told them that all the men had returned. Two of the vaqueros had been wounded lightly, but their broad smiles showed how proud they were of their bloody bandages.

The women began to shout with joy and with as much triumph as the riders. Gabe was reminded of an Oglala war party returning to the village . . . except for the lack of scalps. The men dismounted, embraced wives, mothers, sisters, children. As usual, the return of warriors had already sparked a great deal of physical passion, the urge to start new life amidst the threat of death. There was no mistaking the looks in the eyes of some of the women as they walked away, arm in arm, with their men. Gabe watched Jorge lead his wife over to his adobe, then shut the door in the faces of his children. Perhaps a baby would be made today. Perhaps, throughout the ranch, many babies.

Gabe did not at first notice Mercedes among the welcoming group. He'd just finished tying his horse to a hitching rack when he turned and saw her, standing about six feet away, looking at him intently. He was struck by the expression of wonderment on her face. "I was afraid you would not return," she said in a low voice. "That you would be killed. Because you are so brave."

"Well, I wasn't," he replied a little awkwardly. He took a step toward her, noticing now that besides wonderment, there was a smoldering quality in the way she was looking at him.

They stood a yard apart. Nothing more was said. By silent agreement they walked away together, heading for the same grove of trees where they'd been when Pedro had ridden into the ranch yard, wounded.

She led him through the trees to the banks of a small stream. The banks were grassy and level. She turned to face him. "Please," she murmured.

He did not have to ask what she wanted. He pulled her into his arms. Her body felt warm, solid against his. Once again, their lips met in a kiss. The kiss began a little hesitantly, but quickly grew more and more passionate.

The engagement was announced that night. If they'd waited until the next day, it might have caused trouble. When the two lovers came back from the woods, the disarray of Mercedes's clothing, the bits of grass clinging to the back of her dress, the deep flush of her skin, was enough to tell any observers all they needed to know. Gabe and Mercedes were now *novio* and *novia*. Betrothed. And God help him if he'd tried to back out of it.

As Mercedes had promised, Jorge was delighted. As was Don Andres. "New blood is always a good thing," he said sagely. "In the old days, there were so few of us here in California, there was always the danger of . . . well, weakening the strain."

In addition to new blood, El Rancho de Las Palomas was also gaining a proven warrior. Gabe was a little abashed at all the attention. He had thought, considering the Latin emphasis on virginity, that Mercedes would have been ostracized for what they had so obviously been doing in the woods. But their future intentions seemed to legitimize her actions. Gabe suspected that these people had been cut off from their mother country for so long a time that old ways, old mores, had

had to bend a little. A frontier mentality had developed.

Mercedes was delighted with her new love. And eager. Very eager. Gabe quickly realized that he had caught a tiger. They met frequently in the woods on their little grassy patch. Soon, Mercedes began to crawl in through the window of his room. They made love on his bed. He wondered why her wild cries brought no one running. Perhaps Don Andres had decided to develop selective hearing.

The visits to his room became frequent. One night, after they had made love, Mercedes raised herself on her elbow and looked over at Gabe. They were very relaxed with one another by now. "You were really raised by the Indians?" she asked.

He shook his head. "I wasn't raised by the Indians. I *was* an Indian. An Oglala. Part of the Lakota nation. What the White Man call the Sioux."

Now it was Mercedes's turn to shake her head. "You don't look at all like an Indian."

He traced his finger over her nose. She blinked. "Like I told you," he said. "My mother and father were both white. Adam and Amelia Conrad, from St. Louis."

"Then . . . they lived with the Indians."

A slight frown creased Gabe's features. "My mother did. She brought me up . . . as an Oglala. My father was killed by the Oglala before I was born."

"And your mother *lived* with them?"

His finger dropped lower, tracing her lips. Full, ripe lips. "She didn't have much choice," Gabe said gently. "After they killed my father, they took her with them. She was already pregnant with me. Had been pregnant for maybe ten minutes."

Her eyes grew large. She looked confused. So he told her how his mother and father, travelling west with a wagon train bound for Oregon, had talked some others into leaving the other wagons and detouring into the Black Hills. Word had been spreading that there was gold in the Black Hills.

"I hated my father for years," Gabe said. "After my mother told me what he'd done. I was disgusted because he'd risked my mother's life because of greed for gold.

And it was a big risk. The Black Hills were sacred to the Oglala and to the Cheyenne. They resented any intrusions. My mother and father's party were camped one morning, when they were attacked by the Bad Faces. That's a subgroup of the Oglala, who are a subgroup of the Lakota Nation. All of the whites were killed except my mother. They might have killed her too, but even after everyone else was dead, she was trying to reload a rifle. She was going to keep on fighting until she was killed. That impressed one of the Oglala, a man named Little Wound. The Oglala value courage. He spared my mother's life, took her with him, made her his woman."

Mercedes shuddered. "How terrible for her."

Gabe shrugged. "Yes, I suppose it was. At least at first. She told me she tried to run away several times, but they always caught her. Eventually, she accepted it. Made Little Wound a good wife."

A slight hesitation. "And . . . you?"

Gabe smiled. "Just before the attack on the wagon train, my mother and father woke up. They made love. She was pregnant with me by the time the attack happened. I was born among the Oglala to a woman who had, in many ways, become an Oglala. I was raised just like any other Oglala boy. Of course, when I got older, I wondered why my hair and eyes were such a different color from everybody else's. My mother was different, too. She had beautiful golden hair. You know how children are, they hate to feel different, but she fixed that for me by saying that the sun had fallen from the sky and given us some of his color and strength. She tried to make me into a perfect little Oglala."

Mercedes shifted her weight a little. "You must have had an Indian name, then."

Gabe hesitated a moment, finally said, "Yes. I did."

Excited eyes. "Come on . . . tell me."

"Long Rider."

She looked puzzled. "Why?"

"When I was fourteen," he told her, "word came that a large group of white soldiers would be riding through the country where some people friendly to us were camped. They had to be warned to get out of the way, and I was the one chosen to warn them. I rode two days and two nights through a terrible blizzard. Killed two horses. But I got there. That's when I got my manhood name—Long Rider—because of that long, hard ride."

He mused a moment, half-smiling. "And it sure was a long ride."

"But your mother called you Gabe."

He shook his head. "Uh-uh. I was called after my Oglala stepfather at first, Little Wound. You see, she figured we'd spend the rest of our lives among the Lakota. There were no whites out there then, just a few trappers. It was only later, when I went to live among the whites, that I got my White Man's name. She named me after an old friend of hers, the mountain man, Jim Bridger. They used to call him Old Gabe. So I became young Gabe. Gabe Conrad. But I told you how I came to leave the People."

Mercedes got up off the bed, began to prowl around the room. She was naked, and Gabe lay back, hands behind his head, admiring her body. A beautiful woman.

At first, she'd been nervous about being naked in front of him. Now she was used to it, even seemed to delight in it, as if it was something they shared that no one else shared with them. He had no complaints.

As a future wife, perhaps trying out the role, she began to examine his possessions, what little there was of them. His duster was hanging on the wall, where it had been for some time; he'd taken to wearing the local short jacket when he worked. She spotted something dark beneath the duster. She pulled the duster away, revealing a long, dark leather coat, with bright pigments painted across its back. "What's this?" she asked.

He felt a touch of annoyance, as if his privacy had been invaded. But this woman was to be his wife. He'd better get used to it. "A coat my mother made. Out of buffalo hides. Before she died."

Mercedes took the duster away and spread the coat out. The picture of a stylized bird had been painted across the back. The outstretched wings reached out over the coat's shoulders. "That bird is called *Wakinyan*," Gabe said, anticipating her question. "What the White Man calls the Thunderbird."

Her Catholic soul was shocked. "A pagan god? An idol?"

He smiled. "A . . . well, something that belongs in nature. A force. A . . . spirit, I suppose."

She looked straight at him. "And you . . . believe in this . . . *Wakinyan*?"

He looked straight back. "An Oglala would never put it that way. 'Believing in' is a white man's idea. The Oglala, or most people they call Indians, would be more likely to just . . . feel something. Sense that it's there, *know* without bothering about believing and not believing, without trying to figure everything out or create some kind of structure. When I returned to the Oglala, after I got out of the stockade, I was longing for that kind of feeling. I went to my spirit mentor, an old man named High Backbone. I told him that now that I returned to the People, I wanted to go on a spirit quest. I had been among the whites so long, their slave, and later their prisoner, that I felt my soul had been damaged. I . . . wanted to look for my spirit again. I wanted to find out where I was."

She looked a little abashed. "Well . . . did you find out?"

He nodded. "Yes. I did."

He told her how he had sat on a hilltop for four days and nights, with no food. Four days of emptiness, until he had finally become convinced that the spirits had abandoned him, that his time among the whites had made him unfit, unclean.

Then, at the very end, he had heard the beating of great wings and had looked up to see *Wakinyan* descending toward him. Those great wings had settled around his shoulders, and as they did, he felt a sense of strength flood through his being. A sense of being protected, powerful, able.

*Wakinyan* had shown him many things. Shown him that he would leave the People and ride apart, on his own lonely path. Had shown him his mother's death. Had made of him a man, a warrior.

Gabe pointed toward the winged figure on the back of the coat. "*Wakinyan* was the central part of my vision," he explained. "When I returned to the village, my mother, who had become more Oglala than she realized, was proud that such a powerful spirit had appeared to me, so she painted *Wakinyan*, as part of the design on a new lodge cover she was making. That was just a few days before the soldiers attacked."

Gabe fell silent for a moment, remembering. Finally, he shook himself. "After the attack, the soldiers burned the village, burned all the lodges, and the winter food, so that the People would die of hunger and exposure during the cold. After the soldiers left, I came back. One of the few things left was this part of the lodge cover. Just the part with the Thunderbird. I took that as a sign, so I cut away the burnt portions, and made this coat out of what was left."

His voice had grown distant. Mercedes hung the duster over the Thunderbird coat. Now her nakedness made her look defenseless. She looked at Gabe gravely. "You sound like a pagan, Gabe. Maybe later after we're married, you'll feel more like a Christian."

For a moment he was annoyed. Then he felt a wave of tenderness sweep over him for this girl who had given herself so openly to him. He smiled. "Maybe," he replied gently.


It was late that same day, when Gabe, alone, climbed a hill about a quarter of a mile from the ranch. He was carrying a long slender bundle, wrapped in deer hide.

He'd noticed the hill not long after he'd come to the ranch. There was something about its shape, its position in the landscape, that had called to him. It looked like the right place for a man to smoke his pipe.

When he reached the top of the hill, his eyes fell on a level spot of ground. That particular area gave him a good feeling; he knew it was the right spot. He sat down cross-legged, placing the bundle in front of him. Then he spent a moment looking around. Yes, the place was good. From where he sat he could see nothing made by man, just sky and trees and distant hills. There was only himself and the earth.

He unwrapped the deer hide, revealing a long Indian pipe. The stem was made of a hollowed-out piece of willow. The bowl had been carved from a soft red stone. It was sacred stone, from Minnesota, where the Oglala had lived before they'd moved out onto the plains. Gabe had been given the pipe while he'd still been in the fort's guardhouse. It had been a gift from an old Oglala medicine man named Two Face—just minutes before the soldiers took Two Face out and hanged him. For nothing. Well, for having sex with a white woman Two Face had rescued from another tribe. The white woman and the soldiers had called it rape. Two Face had thought of it much more simply. After all, he'd rescued the woman, and what else were women for?

Gabe had kept the pipe ever since. He used it in times like this, when he was confused, when he needed to communicate with those mysterious forces that lie all around mankind, but cannot be seen, only felt.

Gabe opened a small pouch and took out the smoking mixture, *chanshasha*, made out of tobacco and dried willow bark. When he had filled the pipe's bowl he sat quietly for a moment, holding the bowl in his left hand, the stem in his right. Then he presented the pipe, first to the spirits of the west, then the north, east, and south. Next, he held the bowl down toward the earth, and finally, up toward the sky.

When it came time to smoke, he cheated. He should have built a small fire, which would have provided him with a coal to light the pipe, but he didn't want smoke from the hilltop to give him away; he was still close to the ranch buildings. So he used a match. When the mixture was burning well, he began to smoke, and as he drew in the pungent smoke, he could feel power flowing into his body along with the smoke. Power and a sense of peace.

As he smoked the rest of the bowlful of *chanshasha*, he began to feel more at ease about what he was about to do. Marry this Spanish girl, make a life for himself at El Rancho de Las Palomas. Join the White Man's religion. Well, the local version of it. Or at least, outwardly do so, because he doubted in his heart that he would ever really become part of that religion. He knew that the whites, all versions of whites, considered the Indians to be savages, considered their beliefs to be pagan ignorance. So be it. But, during all Gabe's travels among the whites he had yet to discover anything the whites believed in that had more to offer than what he had learned as an Oglala.

So he would live here among these people. They were good people. He loved Mercedes; he wanted to wake up each morning with her lying beside him. But, whenever he felt his spirit bogging down within the White Man's heavy, grim view of the world, he would come here to this hilltop. He would sit privately and smoke his pipe. He would honor *Wakan-tanka*, what the White Men called the Great Spirit, but which Gabe, like most Indians, saw simply as all that mysteriousness out there, the foundation of the universe. Unknowable to the human mind. The mystery of life, of the world itself. A mystery any intelligent man would try to communicate with, even if he could not fully understand it. Not seek it out inside some dark church, full of images of suffering and death, but outside, under the sky, sitting on the earth itself, open, ready.

Deep in his heart, he would always be Long Rider, the fourteen-year-old boy who had gained his name by riding to warn his people of danger.

# CHAPTER FOURTEEN

They found the first dead cow about three miles from the ranch. It had bloated in the sun and stank badly. Gabe put his bandanna over his mouth and nose before he got down from his horse to examine the corpse. There were no visible wounds, so one of the vaqueros dabbed his reata loop around a stiffened leg and turned the animal over.

Still no visible sign of death. Then Gabe noticed a greenish froth around the animal's muzzle. "Are there any bad water holes around here?" he asked the other men.

They shook their heads and shrugged. They did not seem particularly concerned. A dead cow was a dead cow.

Then they found three more dead animals, all within a radius of a few hundred yards. All without signs of violent death. Now some of the men began to grow a little concerned. Perhaps some kind of plague, God's curse, had broken loose within their herds. Which would be a disaster. The whole herd could be wiped out, and with it, El Rancho de Las Palomas.

Gabe noticed buzzards spiraling in the air not too far away. He rode in that direction. Two more dead cows. Yet, the buzzards were not touching them. That began to give him ideas.

He found the salt block sitting in a small clearing. It had already been licked partly shapeless. A dead coyote lay only a few yards from the salt block. Dismounting, Gabe saw the same greenish froth on the coyote's muzzle.

One of the vaqueros had an old piece of tarp tied behind his saddle. Gabe borrowed the tarp, gingerly rolled the salt block into it, tied the bundle tightly, and hung it over his mount's haunches, back of the saddle.

He rode straight back to the ranch, leaving the other men to look for more dead cattle. When he reached the ranch yard, he dumped the salt block in a shed, then went into the main house. Don Andres and Jorge were seated around a table. Gabe noticed that they already wore worried expressions, and he had not yet told them about the cattle.

"What's the matter?" he asked.

"We had visitors," Jorge replied. "Two men. One of them said something about taxes. They are going to reappraise the ranch, something like that; we didn't really understand, but it will cost money."

"And the other man," Don Andres said drily, "was from that man, Barnes. He made me another offer to buy the ranch. A slightly better offer this time, but still very low. As if I would sell for any price."

Figuring he might as well get it over with, Gabe told them about the dead cattle. Don Andres looked stricken. "Hoof-and-mouth disease?" he asked, his face gray. If it was hoof-and-mouth, anthrax, the law would require him to destroy his whole herd and burn the bodies. He would be wiped out.

"I don't think so," Gabe replied. He told them about the salt block. Don Andres abruptly stood up. "We shall see," he said, heading toward the door.

They took the salt block to a small corral and set it down on the ground inside. A sick old goat, with little time to live, was put into the corral with the block. It immediately began to lick the block, eager for the salt. Don Andres, Jorge, and Gabe stood watching.

It did not take long; the goat was much smaller than a cow, not a whole lot larger than the dead coyote Gabe had found. Within five minutes the goat was having trouble standing. Its leg shook, it staggered in circles, and finally fell. A few last convulsions, and it was dead. Even from outside the corral the men could see the greenish froth around its mouth.

"A poisoned salt block," Jorge murmured angrily. "Those *hijos de putas*. No telling how many more they may have placed."

A small bell tower rose up near the house. Jorge went over to it, began to pull hard on a rope. The bell tolled loudly. Within minutes, vaqueros began to ride into the yard from every direction, while the people still at the ranch came running out of their houses.

Don Andres sat down on a chopping block. "Barnes," he said tightly. "it has to be him. He is attacking my cattle . . . to force me to sell. And trying to frighten me about taxes."

More men rode in. Jorge detailed them to search over every part of the range, looking for salt blocks. "The trouble is," he told Gabe, "we can't tell which are the good ones that we placed, and which are the ones that belong to Barnes. We'll have to get rid of them all. And when we place new ones, how can we tell whether more poisoned ones have been smuggled in?"

It took two days to bring in all the salt blocks. Fortunately, no more dead cattle were found. Perhaps the block Gabe had found had been the only poisoned one.

Now, new troubles surfaced. One Saturday evening, three of the vaqueros came riding back to the ranch, bloodied and battered. One had been so badly beaten that he could barely sit his horse. They had left the ranch two hours before, on their way to a cantina about ten miles away on the main wagon road. They told a story of six white men, gunmen, who had pulled pistols on them, taken away their own arms, then beaten them for a quarter of an hour. They had been given a message, a greeting to their *patrón* from someone who was a great admirer of Don Andres, and of El Rancho de Las Palomas.

Barnes again. It had to be Barnes. "We should hunt those men down," Gabe said to Don Andres. "Either hurt them badly or kill them. And if it happens again, go after Barnes. Kill him, too."

For the first time since they'd met, Gabe saw Don Andres look confused. "Perhaps that is what they want us to do," the old man said. "Have us go after Barnes's men . . . if they are indeed his men, and not simply some gunmen riding through. And if they are, and we kill them, what then? A friend of mine had a similar problem. When he fought back, the law was brought in. He was thrown into the *juzgado*, and while he was there, a lawsuit was started. He lost everything."

"You can't just let them whittle you away, piece by piece."

Don Andres nodded. He was looking a little more decisive now. "No, we cannot. We will keep an eye on those six men. In addition, our vaqueros will ride now only in groups large enough to defend themselves. And, if the trouble continues, we will do as you suggest, we will go after this man, Barnes, and kill him. Better to lose everything after a good fight than to lose it lying down, whimpering like a sick dog."

Gabe nodded, but as he walked away with Jorge, he murmured to his friend, "We ought to ride down to that cantina right now. Take care of those six hombres."

"True," Jorge agreed. "But we will give it a little time. Make sure what is happening."

Gabe shook his head. "Sometimes you're only sure after you're dead."

Don Andres ordered a man to keep watch on the cantina. Sure enough, the six men were staying there. And they did indeed look like gunmen. Don Andres gave orders that none of his men were to go near the place, except the watcher, who remained carefully hidden on a hilltop overlooking the cantina. Gabe lent him his binoculars.

Meanwhile, they would have to get their supplies from a trading post much further away, in the opposite direction. The ranch produced most of the things it needed, but there were some items that it was easier to purchase or trade for. One morning, a wagon was readied. A steer had been butchered, and some of the meat was to be taken to the trading post to exchange for hardware, flour, cloth, and other necessities.

Mercedes demanded that she be allowed to go along. "I want to buy some ribbons and lace for my wedding clothes," she told Jorge, when he at first refused. "No, I don't want the men to pick them out for me," she insisted. "I have to do it myself."

Finally, Jorge agreed. But he decided to go along. "For your protection," he told his sister.

They set out a little after ten in the morning. Mercedes rode in the wagon, while Jorge and another man rode alongside. It was a beautiful sunny day, but a little cold, with a slight threat of rain later on, and as the wagon jolted along the rough trail, Mercedes's heart was full of joy. In just a few days, she would be married. She and Gabe would be given a house of their own in which to live. Together. They would lie side by side every night and wake up close together in the morning. Her handsome, gray-eyed warrior would make babies with her. Lots of babies.

How lucky she'd been. From the time she'd been a little girl, she'd expected that someday she would marry one of the local men. But over the years she had not found any she wanted. There was nothing wrong with them; some were handsome enough, some were witty and full of life, but they were all of the same kind as herself, the same land. From the time she'd been a little girl, she'd realized that she wanted something different, something that would bring adventure and change into her life. And now it had happened. She had a man who was different from any man she'd ever met. A man she respected even over the *patrón*.

She'd never thought Gabe would want to marry her. She'd recognized the wanderlust in him from the day they'd met, was sure he would simply ride away one day. Disappear. But she'd wanted him, could not help herself, and, marvelously, he had decided he wanted her. She'd made him notice her, made him realize that she was the woman for him, because she, too, shared some of that wanderlust. Perhaps someday they would ride away together, search out adventures. And then, of course, they would return to El Rancho de Las Palomas to tell the others about those adventures. Because Mercedes could not imagine a life without her birthplace, her friends, her brother, her own land as part of that life, at least part of the time. Yes, perhaps they would travel. And, travelling or at home, make love day after day. She shivered with pleasure as she remembered the last time they'd made love, the things Gabe had done to her.

She was still daydreaming when she heard Jorge utter an exclamation. The wagon jolted to a halt. Mercedes looked up, then froze. Three mounted men were blocking the trail, about thirty yards ahead.

Jorge had seen them the moment they rode out of the brush. Gunmen. Americanos. Lots of rifles and pistols. He looked around quickly. Sure enough, there were three more, two off to one side, above the trail, and one on the other side.

Jorge glanced at the vaquero riding on the far side of the wagon. Be ready, Jorge's eyes said. But the man had only an old pistol, and the wagon driver was unarmed. Jorge had his Winchester, but the men from El Rancho de Las Palomas were woefully outgunned by the Americanos. He knew the six gunmen were here to cause trouble. He'd like to avoid that trouble, but he'd be damned before he'd let them beat him, the way the three vaqueros had been beaten at the cantina.

Then he realized. Oh God, why had he let Mercedes talk him into letting her come along?

One of the gunmen blocking the trail rode out ahead of the other two. "Where you headed, greasers?" he asked.

"Straight to hell," another of the gunmen said, snorting with laughter. "Hey, Jed. . . . good lookin' girl they got with 'em. A little bonus."

"Please move from the trail," Jorge said tightly. "You are blocking our way."

The man who'd laughed before, now giggled. "The greaser's catchin' on, Jed. He thinks we're blockin' 'em. Hell, that ain't nothin' compared to what we're gonna do, is it?"

The man named Jed shook his head slowly. "Uh-uh, Charlie. Hey, I see what you mean about the girl. She's gonna be fun. After we take care o' those three yahoos with her."

Mercedes felt a cold chill seep through her body. Oh God, if only Gabe were here. As she thought of Gabe,

despair intensified the chill inside her. If these men did
to her what she thought they wanted to do, maybe Gabe
wouldn't want her anymore. She'd be dirty, defiled.
"Jorge," she half-whispered to her brother. "Don't let
them . . . do things to me."

Jorge nodded. If only he had not let her talk him into taking
her along, he thought again. But he had, and she was right.
No matter what else happened, he must not let these grinning
scum dirty his sister. No matter what it cost him personally.
"Paco," he said in a steady voice. "Now."

Jorge was already sliding his Winchester from its saddle
scabbard. Paco, a little slower, began to reach for his pistol.

"Jesus!" one of the gunmen shouted.

Jorge and Paco never had a chance. Jorge barely had time
to lever a round into the chamber and start to aim, when the
first bullet hit him. It was the men to the sides of the trail who
caused the most initial damage. Their bullets caught Jorge
and Paco in a deadly cross fire, slamming into their bodies,
knocking them half out of their saddles, and then Jed and
Charlie and the other man in the middle of the trail opened
up, and Jorge and Paco were knocked from their horses by a
fusillade of bullets. The driver, terrified, tried to stand up and
jump from the wagon, but one of the men shot him through
the head. Jorge and Paco's riderless mounts, neighing loudly, immediately broke and ran.

Which left only Mercedes. And the six gunmen. She
had no doubt about what they would do to her. Her body
shuddered with dread as she imagined the rape. And, since
she'd seen them gun down Jorge and the others, she knew
they wouldn't permit her to live.

Not that she would want to live. Not dishonored. Not after
having watched her brother die for her. She suddenly vaulted
from the wagon. Jorge's rifle had fallen to the ground. She
bent low, picked it up. It felt heavy in her hands. She wished
she'd paid more attention when he'd tried to show her how
to use it. Work the lever, she reminded herself, unaware that
there was already a shell in the chamber, that the rifle was
ready to fire.

A bright brass shell flew through the air as she jerked at the loading lever. Another slid into the firing chamber.

"Put down that rifle, you stupid bitch!" Jed shouted.

But she was already raising the Winchester, pointing it at Jed. She noticed he had a pistol in his hand. She fired. And missed. Jed cursed as the bullet whistled past his head. "I said put it down!" he shouted again.

But Mercedes was already working the lever. Another shell loaded. She was raising the rifle again, when Jed sighted his pistol at her and pulled the trigger.

Mercedes felt an enormous blow strike her chest. She was vaguely aware of flying backward, aware that she no longer held the rifle. She fell full length on her back, in the middle of the trail. The impact puffed up a small cloud of dust around her body.

She tried to breathe, but her lungs would not work. "Goddamn, Jed," she heard one of the men say disgustedly. "You done gone and killed one o' the nicest looking pieces I seen in a month o' Sundays."

Mercedes knew, then, that she was dying. Her lungs still wouldn't work, and pain seemed to be lurking somewhere in the background. But the pain, alongside with everything else, was being pushed further and further away from her. Dark. Darkness all around, except for one point, one intensely bright spot, directly in front of her eyes.

As Mercedes stared up at the sun, dying, a terrible sadness swept over her. There would be no wedding, no long years of happiness. Never, never again, would she and Gabe lie together in one another's arms.

# CHAPTER FIFTEEN

Gabe was less than half a mile from the ranch, chasing cattle, when he heard the alarm bell ringing. He and the two men with him immediately whipped up their horses and dashed toward the sound of the bell.

When they rode into the ranch yard, a knot of people had already formed around a man standing next to a lathered horse. Gabe recognized the man as the one who'd been chosen to keep watch over the cantina.

Gabe looked around, searching for Mercedes. He did not see her. She was usually one of the first. . . .

A slow dread began to build inside Gabe, intensified when he saw the horrified, pitying looks that many of those present were casting in his direction.

Gabe immediately rode up to Don Andres and slipped from his saddle, so that he was standing very close to the old man. "What is it? What's happened?" Gabe demanded.

The look Don Andres gave him was full of grief. "Mercedes," he said in a low, broken voice. "Jorge. Dead. Killed by those Americano gunmen."

Gabe stood totally still. He felt very cold, unable to move. Ice seemed to be forming inside him. Finally, he was able to speak. "Where?" he demanded. "How?" His voice sounded distant to him, as if he were shouting into a tunnel.

Don Andres gestured toward the man who'd been on guard duty at the cantina. "Diego . . ." he said softly. "He saw . . ."

Gabe spun toward Diego, who blanched and turned away, unnerved by the total lack of expression in Gabe's eyes, the total coldness. "Tell me," Gabe said tersely.

Diego swallowed. "I was watching the cantina this morning," he said haltingly. "One of the gunmen had ridden out earlier. Then he came riding back, fast. He went inside. There was a lot of shouting, then the others came outside. They all mounted and rode out toward the main trail."

Don Andres cut in. "One of them must have been watching the trail that runs from here to the trading post. They can see anyone coming down the mountainside from at least a mile away. He saw the wagon, Mercedes and Jorge. . . ."

"Yes," Diego said. "He must have seen the wagon coming down the mountain. I knew nothing about it, and I had to keep well back, out of sight, so they would not know I was following them. I heard gunfire, lots of it, and rode hard toward a hilltop that overlooks the trail. That's when I saw . . ."

Diego was having trouble continuing. "They were standing there . . . all six of those pigs were standing over the bodies. I . . . I looked through your binoculars, Gabe. I . . . they all looked very dead. Then I rode back here, for help. . . ."

"But you're not sure they're dead," Gabe snapped. He turned toward the others. "Damn it! Why aren't you all in the saddle?"

His anger seemed to galvanize the others into action. Men ran into their houses, picked up guns, came running back out, heading toward the usual group of waiting saddle horses. By then, Gabe was already out of the ranch yard, riding hard toward the main trail.

He could hear others riding after him. He turned in the saddle once, saw a ragged line of a dozen men strung out behind him. He turned back toward the front, not wanting them to see his face, afraid that it might betray the agony tearing at his insides. Mercedes. What had she been doing in a wagon so far from the ranch? And Jorge. His friend. They couldn't be dead. Diego had probably panicked. Perhaps they were just hurt.

Then a terrible thought occurred to him. Perhaps Mercedes had been . . . Perhaps the men had . . .

He did not let himself finish the thought, fought to keep his emotions under control, unaware that his face showed nothing at all of his inner feelings. Young Oglala were trained from childhood to mask their feelings, to never show pain, never let anyone see their agony. Even an agony as great as this.

Riding down out of the hills, he could see the wagon below. And the bodies on the ground around it. He glanced up. Vultures were circling lazily, which gave him hope that there was at least some life remaining below, keeping the vultures at bay.

But as he rode closer, his hope died. Too much blood. Way too much blood. He slipped from his horse next to Mercedes's body. She lay on her back, arms at her sides, staring up at the sun through half-open eyes. Her white blouse was soaked in blood. More blood had pooled beneath her body, soaking into the ground.

Gabe cast a quick glance at Jorge, who lay a few feet away. Shot to pieces. No hope there. He turned back toward Mercedes.

By now, the others had ridden up. Men dismounted, checked the bodies of Paco and the driver. Gabe could hear from the hushed voices that there was no life there, either.

He remained standing over Mercedes, looking down at her. She looked almost normal, as if she had not died in pain. Her lips were slightly parted, her hair was spread out around her head, and, as he had already noticed, her eyes were partly open. He bent a little. There was no light in those eyes. No light, no love, no feeling. Nothing. Only death.

Gabe noticed that Jorge's Winchester lay alongside Mercedes. He picked it up, sniffed the barrel, smelled gun smoke. He knew then that Mercedes had gone down fighting. He was able to take a little comfort from that, but not much.

He threw the rifle into the wagon, then bent down, got his arms beneath Mercedes, and picked her up. Her arms and legs were limp, her head lolled. She was already cold to the touch. Gently, he laid her inside the wagon, straightened her skirt around her legs, tried to smooth out her sticky, blood-soaked blouse. He took one last look at her face, her beautiful, peaceful face, then turned away, heading toward his horse.

Some of the riders were already putting the other bodies into the wagon. One man came up to Gabe. His face was bleak, barely able to contain the anger he felt. He laid a hand on Gabe's shoulder just as Gabe was about to mount. "Wait another minute or two," he said to Gabe. "One man can take the . . . bodies back to the ranch. The rest of us will ride with you."

Gabe turned. The vaquero backed away from the look on Gabe's face. "If anyone tries to follow me to the cantina," Gabe said in a flat, hard voice, "I'll kill him. I ride alone."

They all watched him mount, then ride away, back straight, eyes forward. A couple of men started toward their horses. The vaquero who'd spoken to Gabe held up a warning hand. "He means it," he snapped. "He'll kill you. This is his thing to do. His personal *venganza*. No one must interfere."

"But," one man protested. "It's six against one. They'll kill him."

The vaquero shook his head. "Perhaps," he replied, turning to watch Gabe's diminishing figure. "And perhaps not."

When he was half a mile from the cantina, Gabe had a fleeting thought of riding up onto high ground, to the place where Don Andres's man had been keeping watch, so that he could scout the area. The thought lasted only a fraction of a second. He continued straight on, as if some force were pushing him to the confrontation with the men who had killed his woman.

He had one other thought, remembering that he had washed this morning, washed his whole body, after having made love to Mercedes the night before. Good. Almost as if he'd somehow known. For a man to ride into a fight, unwashed, after having made love to a woman, was to invite death.

He felt ready for whatever lay ahead. He had an actual physical sensation of *Wakinyan* hovering somewhere above him. He looked up. There was nothing tangible to see, but he knew that the Winged One was there, he could feel his presence.

The cantina lay just ahead. It was a sagging log structure, about half again as long as it was wide, sitting in the middle of a dirty, cluttered yard, with rickety outbuildings nearby. As Gabe rode into the yard, he noticed six saddled horses tied near the front door. A Mexican man, probably in his forties, was scattering feed to half a dozen chickens. He looked up as Gabe rode into the yard, but when he saw Gabe dismount and slip his Winchester from its saddle scabbard and start toward the front door, most of all, when he saw the look on Gabe's face, the cold, ready-to-kill intensity of that look, he dropped what feed remained and ran in the opposite direction.

There was a small, dirty window set near the front door. The window was partly open. Gabe could hear voices coming from inside. A man was saying, "I think we oughta get the hell outta here, Jed. Those greasers up at the ranch are gonna find the bodies sooner or later. And then they're gonna come after us. I bet they could get together twenty men."

A nasal voice, with a Southern drawl replied. Probably Jed. "They ain't got the guts, Charlie. Besides, handlin' twenty o' those gutless bastards wouldn't be no trouble a'tall. We was paid to stay here and cause that spic rancher lots of grief, an' that's what we been doin'."

Another voice cut in, a low, faintly amused voice. "Hell, you caused *me* some grief, Jed, when you shot that girl. If you hadn't o' done that, we'd all o' been having one hell of a lot of fun right now."

The man had time to say no more. Gabe kicked the front door open and leveled his rifle. He had an instant image of six

men, sitting and standing around a cluttered room, all turning toward the door, surprise on their faces. From where the
voices had been coming from, Gabe was certain that the man
who'd made the comments about Mercedes was the one sitting closest to the front door. "Woman killers," Gabe said in
a flat voice, then proceeded to pump two .44 caliber rounds
into the man's body.

The man had already started to stand up. The bullets
knocked him over the back of his chair. He hit the floor
with a loud crash.

"Jesus!" Gabe heard one man shout.

The room exploded into action as the five remaining men
clawed for their guns. As Gabe had expected, they were all
experienced killers, and all were reacting with tremendous
speed.

Hammers clicked back, but by then Gabe had ducked to
the right, away from the door, just an instant before eight or
ten shots shattered the door frame.

Time to move. As he'd been riding up, Gabe had noticed
there was another window, in the side wall of the cantina.
Running soundlessly in his moccasins, he raced toward the
window. There was a lot of shouting from inside the cantina.

"Tom's dead!" one man called out.

"Let's get the bastard!" another man shouted back.

"Wait!" a voice commanded. "Take it slow. He may be
waitin' right outside the door."

Gabe was pretty sure this last voice belonged to the one
they'd called Jed. The one who'd killed Mercedes. By then,
Gabe had reached the side window. He took just a moment
to peer inside. He saw men milling around, all with guns
in their hands. He broke the window with the muzzle of
his rifle, fired three fast shots, saw men go scrambling for
cover, saw the head of one man explode.

As with the front door, bullets tore chunks out of the window frame, but Gabe was already racing toward the rear of
the building . . . where he ran straight into one of the gunmen, a fast thinker who'd run out the back door to ambush
him.

They collided hard. The gunman's pistol went flying, but he managed to get both hands on Gabe's Winchester, so that Gabe could not bring the muzzle around toward him. The two men stood swaying for a moment, fighting for possession of the rifle.

"I got him! Gimme a hand!" the man shouted.

Jed again. The one who'd killed Mercedes. Rage gave Gabe sudden strength. He suddenly stepped forward. Jed had been yanking on the rifle, and Gabe's unexpected move threw him backward. Gabe was wearing his knife in a sheath toward the back of his belt. While Jed was fighting for balance, Gabe reached behind him with his right hand, seized the handle of his knife, drew it, then drove the long blade deep into Jed's belly.

Jed let out an agonized grunt. Gabe had expected him to let go of the rifle, but the shock of the knife entering his belly caused Jed to hold onto the Winchester even more tightly, hold on desperately.

Gabe ripped the knife sideways, tearing a huge gash in Jed's belly. Blood gushed out over Gabe's hand. Jed screamed, a high-pitched scream of agony. His legs pistoned, throwing him away from that terrible blade. Gabe had to let him go. He watched Jed fall toward the side of the building, taking the rifle with him.

Gabe heard the sound of running feet, coming from both the front and the rear of the cantina. The knife handle was slippery with blood. He let it drop from his hand as he ducked behind a shed. Just in time. A pistol roared. Splinters flew from the side of the shed. Gabe ran from the shed, slipping behind an outhouse, desperately wiping blood from his hand.

Three men. There would be three men left. He slipped his revolver from its belt holster, crouching, listening. He heard the sound of running feet again, two to his right, one to his left, from the direction of the shed.

Gabe stepped out from behind the outhouse just as a lone gunman came around the corner of the shed. The man's drawn pistol was pointing off to one side, but when he saw Gabe, the pistol's muzzle began to rise.

Gabe's pistol was already pointing at the other man. No time to aim, no point in aiming at this range, anyhow. Holding down the trigger with his bent right index finger, both hands wrapped around the butt, Gabe fanned the hammer with his left thumb, sending three bullets into the gunman's chest. He fired so quickly that the three shots sounded like one, drawn-out explosion.

The gunman was still falling when Gabe heard a shout behind him. Then bullets from two pistols were flying his way, but he'd already run past the dying gunman to the far side of the shed.

Boots pounded along after him. Rounding a corner of the shed, Gabe braked to a stop, flattened himself against the building, changed the pistol to his left hand, and held it cocked and waiting.

His pursuer nearly ran into the muzzle. Gabe pulled the trigger, sending a bullet into the man's neck. The gunman staggered backward. Blood jetted from the wound in rhythmic pulses; the bullet must have hit an artery. But the man was still alive, and his pistol was still in his right hand, so Gabe shot him in the head.

A shout of rage from behind. Gabe ducked away just before a bullet creased his left shoulder and slammed into the shed behind him. Thrown off balance by the bullet, feeling as if a white hot branding iron had been laid against his shoulder, Gabe spun away, off balance. He twisted his head around. A man was bearing down on him, a big man. Gabe thrust his pistol beneath his left arm, fired, but he was too far off balance, and the bullet missed, although it passed so close to the other man's face that he flinched away, just as he fired again.

The bullet missed Gabe by a wide margin. Then both men leveled their pistols, the muzzles pointing straight at one another. The distance was only a yard. Wild eyes stared into wild eyes; there would be no missing at this range. Two hammers fell. . . . only to click on already ruptured caps. Both pistols were empty.

Gabe threw his pistol at the other man, then charged in beneath it. The man raised his hands to ward off the pistol, then Gabe was on him, crashing hard against his chest. The man's pistol went flying. They fell to the ground together, clawing at one another.

The man was very strong. He used his head to butt Gabe over the right eye. Gabe's head spun. He was groggy just long enough for the man to roll on top of him. Gabe felt powerful fingers close around his throat. He tensed his neck muscles; he could barely breathe.

The man pounded Gabe's head down against the ground. Gabe tried to twist away, but the hands tightened around his throat, while the man's legs pinned him in place. Gabe saw red, as blood backed up into his eyes.

He knew he had only seconds in which to save himself. If the blood supply to his head was shut off for long enough, even for a few seconds, he would start to black out. Then the man would kill him at his leisure.

Gabe clawed upward, tore at the man's upper lip with his thumb. The man bent his head backward. For just a second the pressure on Gabe's throat lessened. Gabe tried to roll free, but the man was too strong. Those terrible fingers tightened around Gabe's throat again.

But Gabe had discovered that the man did not like having his face mutilated. Gabe clawed upward again. The fingers of his left hand slid along the man's nose, tearing at the nostrils. Gabe felt the slipperiness of blood, and the man's head snapped back.

Gabe was ready when the man leaned forward again, pressing his thumbs deep into Gabe's throat. Gabe's left hand was still against the man's face. He clawed with his index finger, felt the tip catch the outside corner of the man's right eye. He rammed the finger into the eye socket, then pulled outward, feeling slime soak his finger.

Gabe heard a hoarse, horrified scream. Suddenly the man's fingers left Gabe's throat. Choking, trying to breathe, Gabe saw the man sitting astride him, his hands clawing at his face. He continued to scream, and as his hands scrabbled at his face, Gabe saw that his right eye was out of the socket, hanging down over his cheek, held only by the remnants of muscles and nerves.

Gabe slammed his hips sideways, spilling the still-screaming man from his body. Gabe continued the roll, until he was well away. He flinched when his ribs rolled over something long and hard. His hands reached down, came up holding a half-finished ax handle. Nearly three feet of hard hickory.

The man had finally come to grips with the horror of losing an eye, more worried now about saving his life. He was scrabbling on his hands and knees toward a pistol one of his comrades had dropped. Gabe sprang forward, slammed the rough ax handle against the side of the man's head.

The man was knocked over onto his side. Gabe leaped onto his body, evaded the man's arms as he desperately rolled onto his back, then Gabe smashed the center of the hard hickory shaft against the man's throat.

The man gagged. Holding the ends of the ax handle, Gabe pressed down with all his weight. The man's body bucked, and his hands clawed at the wood, trying to shove it away from his throat.

Too late. Gabe pressed harder. Something crunched in the man's throat. His arms flailed wildly as he tried to breathe, but his trachea had been crushed.

His body bucked and jerked beneath Gabe for a little while longer, until a final shudder shook his entire frame. Then he lay still, his chest no longer heaving, no longer attempting to suck in air.

Gabe let go of the ax handle and got shakily to his feet. Six, that should have been the last of the six killers. Nevertheless, he staggered over to retrieve his pistol. His fingers shook as he removed the empty cylinder. The butt of the pistol was slippery with blood. He pulled out his shirttail and wiped some of the blood away. Fumbling in a vest pocket, he took out a loaded cylinder, which he slipped into place inside the revolver's frame. He vaguely noticed that one of the caps was missing, so he turned the cylinder until he was sure that a loaded chamber would come up next.

A horrible scream shattered the silence. Gabe's head jerked around. He automatically pulled back the hammer, but he saw no one. Then the scream sounded again. It was coming from the other side of the shed, near the cantina.

Gabe carefully moved around the shed. He saw movement near the cantina's side wall, then heard a low, agonized moan. It was Jed, the man he'd gutted. He was still alive.

Carefully scanning the area to each side, Gabe walked toward Jed. He was writhing on the ground, with both hands pressed to his body, trying to hold his guts inside his body cavity. Useless.

Jed screamed again. Then he saw Gabe. "Oh God. It hurts," Jed moaned. "Hurts so much."

Gabe moved closer. Jed saw the pistol in his hands. "Please," he whimpered. "Shoot me. Make it stop hurting."

Gabe stood over the man who'd murdered his woman. Half of him wanted to empty his pistol into Jed, savage what was left of his body, the other half wanted to leave him here to die in agony. Jed read the indecision in Gabe's eyes. "Please," he repeated.

The rage left Gabe's face. His expression was unreadable. He knelt close to Jed, then wished he hadn't; the smell was terrible, but he did not back away. "Who sent you?" he asked.

"Please . . . help me," Jed whimpered. "Hurts . . . real bad. So bad."

He screamed again. Gabe stood up, kicked Jed in the side. Jed screamed louder. "I asked you a question!" Gabe shouted. "Who sent you?"

Through a haze of pain, Jed seemed to become aware of what Gabe was saying. He mumbled something. Gabe had trouble understanding; Jed's agony had caused him to bite partway through his lips and tongue. Then Gabe could make out the syllables.

"Barnes," Jed mumbled. "Henry Barnes. Tricky bastard got us all killed. Said they wouldn't fight back. Didn't say nothin' 'bout a white man. . . ."

"Where is he?" Gabe snapped.

Jed looked up into Gabe's remorseless eyes, fought for the words. "Ranch. Got hisself a place . . . near Los Angeles. Up in the hills. Big place. Lotsa men. . . ."

Another terrible scream, then Jed began to rave, cursing, crying, mouthing meaningless sounds. Gabe knew he would get nothing more from him that would be useful. He raised his pistol, put the muzzle inches from Jed's eyes, pulled back the hammer.

Perhaps it was the familiar sound of a revolver being cocked that broke Jed free of his ravings. His eyes cleared for a moment as he stared into the black hole of the gun muzzle.

"That was my woman you killed," Gabe said softly. "And one of the men was her brother, my friend. I want you to know why you're dying, why you hurt so much."

Jed continued to stare into the pistol's muzzle. Before, he'd begged for death. Now, its imminence terrified him. "Oh, God!" he shrieked. He was staring at the twisted first joint of Gabe's index finger, saw it whiten as Gabe applied pressure to the trigger.

The gun bucked in Gabe's hand. The bullet entered at the bridge of Jed's nose, then exited out the back of his skull, spraying the wall of the cantina with brains and blood. Jed flopped onto his back. His legs twitched a few times, then he lay dead.

Gabe stood up, rammed the pistol back into its holster. He looked one last time at Jed's body, then, on shaky legs, he started toward his horse, which was cropping grass fifty yards away. Nervous because of the smell of blood which still clung to Gabe, the horse played coy, backing away several times, until Gabe was able to catch the reins. He steadied the animal, then swung up into the saddle.

One last look around the cantina, the killing ground, then he turned the horse away, toward El Rancho de Las Palomas. He had a woman to bury. Good-byes to say.

Then, another man to kill.

# CHAPTER SIXTEEN

When Gabe got back to the ranch, mourning was in full swing; women were crying, men walked about with stunned looks on their faces, even the dogs looked full of confused grief.

Gabe went straight to Don Andres. The old man was in his study, seated in a massive wooden armchair. He seemed older, shrunken. He looked up when Gabe came in, saw blood on Gabe's left shoulder, the bruises around his throat and face, the blood caking his hands and wrists from when he'd gutted Jed.

"Those men?" Don Andres asked softly.

"They're all dead," Gabe replied, his voice flat, uninflected.

Don Andres nodded slowly. "At too great a price. My God, how am I going to run this place without Jorge? I never had a son. I . . ." Don Andres shook his head. "But I am thinking only of myself. What about you? Mercedes. That lovely girl . . ." He sighed. "I suppose you will leave here now?"

"Yes. I'm going after Barnes. None of this would have happened if it had not been for his greed."

He did not add that it would not have happened if they'd gone after Barnes the moment he began to harass the ranch. The six gunmen would have been dead or run off before they had a chance to kill. And Barnes would not have been around to send more. Never leave an enemy alive. A lesson Gabe had learned long ago.

Don Andres could not meet Gabe's eyes. He was thinking the same thing. "I will be sorry to see you leave," the old man said softly.

Gabe nodded. A month ago, Don Andres would have demanded that he and Gabe go after Barnes together. Now, he simply looked old and beaten. Gabe wondered if he'd be able to hold onto the ranch. Someone else would probably come along, some greedy Americano businessman, and try to take it away. Gabe sighed. Was there never an end to the White Man's greed?

Don Andres insisted that Gabe have his wounds attended to. Not wanting to be slowed by infection, Gabe agreed, but first he went back to his room, got some clean clothing, went down to the stream, and bathed. He bathed next to the spot where he and Mercedes had first made love. He did it on purpose. Remembering the unexpected happiness he'd found with this girl from another culture, he felt his body and mind filling with anger, a desire for revenge. Barnes would pay. He would pay very dearly. His desire for El Rancho de Las Palomas would cost him more than he could ever imagine.

Gabe went back to his room. An old woman came, sent by Don Andres. She cleaned the graze on his shoulder, poured rum over it, then wrapped it in a clean bandage. She had a salve for his bruises and cuts.

By the time Gabe left his quarters, the bodies were on display in the adobe's largest room, washed and dressed by the old women. Jorge, Paco, and the driver were not too easy to look at; bullets had found their faces and heads. But Mercedes . . . someone had finally closed her eyes. She was dressed in a blouse and skirt Gabe had never seen before. She looked almost as if she were asleep, as if at any moment she might spring up and say it was all a joke, a game. But she wouldn't. She would never move again.

Gabe spent the rest of the day cleaning his guns and readying his gear. He ate more for the strength he knew he

would need than for the taste. He had only one goal now.
Barnes.

While the women spent the evening praying over the
corpses, Gabe lay down on his bed. Sleep came in
snatches. Finally, an hour before first light, he got up,
dressed, and walked to his hilltop, carrying the deerskin
bundle containing his pipe. He sat cross-legged, emptying
his mind, waiting for the sun, watching the light grow.
The mountains slowly appeared around him, purple in the
dawn light. The sun rose. Long morning shadows stretched
across meadows where cattle grazed, knee-deep in morning
mist. A beautiful land, but no longer his land.

When the sun finally broke over the eastern peaks, he
had his pipe ready, a small fire going, coals glowing. After
offering the pipe to the six directions, he smoked, and as
the smoke filled him, El Rancho de Las Palomas and its
people began to fade in his mind. Except for one person.
He filled his mind with images of Mercedes and promised
the spirits he would hold her there until the man who'd
caused her death no longer existed.

Coming down from the hill, he went to a corral and roped
his big black stallion. The horse was cantankerous at first;
it had not been ridden much lately, but it soon remembered
who was boss. Gabe led it to a barn, saddled it. He walked
back to his room for his gear, took it to the barn, and strapped
it all into place: rifles, bedroll, saddlebags. Plus something
new. His reata. A gift from Jorge.

He heard the alarm bell tolling, this time softly. He
walked out of the barn. The funerals were already starting.
Four wooden coffins stood on sawhorses under the open
sky. A Spanish priest had been sent for. He intoned words
in a language Gabe did not understand. The congregation
stood in a solemn group until the mass for the dead was
over. Then the coffins were loaded onto a wagon which
would take them to the ranch cemetery, where several
generations of its people were buried.

That was Gabe's cue to leave. All during the mass he'd
been standing well back, present, but not completely par-
ticipating in what was happening. The part that would

follow, he could not bear to see . . . Mercedes lowered into a hole in the ground, then covered with dirt. Trapped, buried. Better the Oglala way, where the dead were placed on a platform, under the open sky, in the fresh air, there to join the elements from which they had come. But the White Men believed human beings were made of mud and dust. Perhaps White Men were.

As the cortege wound its way up toward the cemetery, Gabe walked back to his room. The only item of his still remaining there was the Thunderbird coat. He remembered explaining it to Mercedes. He took it down from its peg, slipped his arms through the sleeves, and as the coat settled into place, with *Wakinyan's* wings spread out over his shoulders, he felt a sense of strength flooding through him, a sense of being protected, invulnerable, powerful. One with the spirits.

He walked to the barn, took his horse outside, and mounted. He took time for one last look at the funeral cortege winding up the little hill toward the cemetery. Then he turned his horse and rode out of the ranch yard. A few of the mourners turned to see him go, a tall man wearing a slouch hat and a long black coat, riding a big black horse.

As he rode away, the sun gleamed on the image of the Thunderbird on the back of the coat. The man who left El Rancho de Las Palomas that morning was no longer Gabe Conrad. He was, once again, Long Rider, Oglala warrior.

# CHAPTER SEVENTEEN

Long Rider headed straight for Los Angeles, retracing the route he'd taken south with Don Andres and Jorge. Not that long ago. The route that had led him to Mercedes.

He spent only one night on the trail, riding into Los Angeles during the evening of the second day. This time he did not check into the Pico House, but chose a small hotel in Sonoratown. He hesitated before going to Dona Amelia's for dinner, but hunger won out. As he'd expected, while he was eating, memories of Jorge came back to haunt him. Memories of himself and Jorge eating at Dona Amelia's, discussing the problems besetting El Rancho de Las Palomas. Once his mind found Jorge, memories of Mercedes lay not far away.

He decided not to fight the memories. They would haunt him for a long time. Perhaps someday, as the pain diminished, they would be memories he'd welcome.

On the way back to his hotel, he tried to decide what he'd do the next morning. Look for Barnes, of course. But where? Jed had claimed that Barnes was living on a ranch. Surrounded by lots of men. Perhaps Barnes was expecting some kind of response from Don Andres, in reply to his harassment. Well, he'd get it.

Another consideration was whether or not to enlist Major Bell's aid. He decided not to. No point involving anyone who would have to live here afterward and answer for the kind of havoc he was about to create.

He got his first break on the way back to the hotel. He was passing through a dark section of street when he saw a man turn into the well-lighted doorway of a bar. For a moment Long Rider was not quite sure where he'd seen the man, but he knew he recognized him. Slowly, bits of memories came back . . . two groups of men facing one another on a dusty trail just south of Los Angeles, the day Don Andres had been wounded in the gunfight with Barnes's hired killers.

Of course. The man Long Rider had recognized was one of the men who'd ridden with Barnes and the Los Angeles mob. The ones who'd been pursuing Don Andres. The man in the bar was the hard-looking man with whom Barnes had conferred before deciding to turn back. Long Rider felt self-contempt rise inside himself as he remembered that day. If he'd only killed Barnes then, Mercedes would still be alive.

There would be no bed tonight, no sleep. Long Rider went back to his room for his gear, which he took to the livery stable. He saddled his horse and put all his gear in place, so that he would be able to ride out at a moment's notice. After a short hesitation, he rented a packhorse, complete with pack-saddle.

He went back out onto the street, then settled down in heavy shadows across the street from the saloon, where he would be able to watch the front door.

The night dragged on, but Long Rider never took his eyes from the saloon door. Finally, at about one in the morning, he saw the same man come out through the doors, staggering a little.

The man turned to the right, walking along the boardwalk. Long Rider conjured up an image of what lay in that direction. *Calle de los Negros.* Dark streets, no one likely to interfere.

He slipped after the man, moving silently from one shadow to the next. Good. His quarry was turning down a narrow dark street. One that Long Rider knew led to whorehouses further along.

Long Rider stopped following and raced down a side

street, just as silently as when he'd been walking. Within a short time he was ahead of his man, lying in wait at the dark mouth of a reeking alleyway.

There. The sound of boots squelching along the foul street. A moment later, a shadowy shape. With perfect timing, Long Rider stepped out of his alleyway and slammed the barrel of his pistol alongside the man's head. The man grunted, swayed for a moment, then fell. Long Rider caught him on the way down, dragging him back into his little alley.

It took less than a minute to bind and gag the man. Leaving him lying in pitch darkness where the man was very unlikely to be found, Long Rider walked quickly back to the livery stable, where he reclaimed both his big stallion and the packhorse. Within minutes he was back in the little alley, bending over his victim. It was hard work, hoisting the man's limp body up and across the packsaddle, but in a little while he had him lashed into place, covered by a tarp.

Long Rider rode straight out of town, using the darkest streets. He headed up into the hills, in a direction where he felt he would find the least amount of people. Within an hour, he heard groans from the man tied across the packsaddle. Paying no attention, Long Rider kept straight on. It was growing light by the time he finally found the kind of place he wanted, a small glade next to a quick, little stream.

By now his captive was cursing and swearing, although disjointedly, not having quite recovered from the blow to his head. Long Rider paid no attention. Dismounting, he began to undress. When he was naked, he took a simple breechclout from his saddlebags and put it on. Digging deeper into the saddlebags, he pulled out some pigments, then spent the next ten minutes looking into a mirror while he painted his face and body in the most warlike colors and patterns he could think of.

Finally, it was time for his captive. The man tried to struggle when Long Rider took him down from the packsaddle. An elbow in the kidneys stiffened the man with pain long enough to get him down and lay him on the ground.

The man knew he was in trouble, he knew he'd been cold-cocked and kidnapped, and that life might start getting even more difficult. If he was to have any life left at all. But, when the tarp was finally pulled aside, he was not prepared for the horrific vision leaning over him—a savage-looking Indian with long sandy hair and incongruously pale eyes. "Jesus!" the man burst out, automatically recoiling. "Who the hell are you?"

Long Rider had already built a small fire, which was quickly burning down to a bed of red hot coals. He dragged his captive closer to the fire, ignoring his questions. Saying nothing, ominously silent, Long Rider pounded four short stakes into the ground. It was not easy tying the man's arms and legs to the stakes, he was obviously waiting for his chance to break free, but with the long blade of his knife constantly in view, Long Rider managed to forestall any dangerous moves.

Finally, he had his captive tied firmly in place, spread-eagled on the ground, near enough to the fire to feel the searing heat of the glowing coals. The man was growing desperate now. "Who the hell are you?" he snarled, trying to hide the fear in his voice. "Why did you bring me here?"

Long Rider knelt down beside the man, and for the first time, looked straight into his face. The man shrank back, fear sweeping through him. He'd never seen such cold, remorseless eyes, and his own eyes were cold enough. A shudder shook his body.

"I saw you with Henry Barnes," Long Rider said, his voice as cold as his eyes.

"Yeah?" the man replied, a little of his defiance returning. "So what?"

"Some of you killed a woman I loved," Long Rider said, if possible even more coldly. "And killed her brother, my friend. Now, you will begin paying for their deaths. All of you. One by one."

"What? I don't know what the hell you're talking about. What woman? What man?"

"Jorge Gonzalez. The *capataz* of El Rancho de Las Palomas. The man who worked for Don Andres Velasquez. And his sister, Mercedes."

Gabe hated saying her name in front of this man, but he was rewarded when he saw partial recognition flare in the man's eyes. "What about them?" the man demanded.

"Some of you, a man named Jed, and five others, killed them," Long Rider replied. "Then I killed Jed, cut his guts out. Killed all six of them. And now I'm going to kill the rest of you."

"What?" the man burst out. "Jed . . . you killed Jed, because he . . . ? But he wasn't s'posed to kill no women. He was just s'posed to . . ."

The man's voice trailed off, as if he knew he'd already said too much. Long Rider turned away, began slowly turning his knife blade over the coals. The man raised his head, watched for a moment, then found his voice again. "Look," he said. "I didn't have nothin' to do with that. I just ride for Barnes, that's all."

Long Rider turned to face him, pinned the man with his cold, emotionless eyes. "That's enough in itself," he said softly. "You'll all have to die. Every man connected with Barnes."

He seemed lost in thought for a moment. "I wonder if you'll scream as loud as Jed did," he finally said, almost absently.

"What . . . what are you gonna do?" the man asked. He was not a soft man, definitely not a coward, but Long Rider's eyes were beginning to get to him. It was their very lack of expression. If they'd been filled with hate or anger, he might have shot back defiance. But there was nothing in those eyes, absolutely nothing he could get a handle on.

Long Rider knelt next to him, a terrifying, painted, half-naked figure, the raw material of a frontiersman's worst nightmare. Probably a white renegade, his captive decided. Everyone knew renegades were twice as bad as real Indians.

The man cringed as this apparition began cutting away his shirt. Long Rider touched the blade to his skin. It was hot, not hot enough to really burn flesh, but hot enough to hurt. The man's body jumped.

"I'm going to take your skin off," Long Rider said in a

matter-of-fact voice. "I'm going to skin you alive, strip by strip. Starting with your chest."

The man turned very pale. "Oh, God, no . . . you can't do that!" he said in a low voice.

But Long Rider continued cutting away the shirt. Finally, he pinched up a fold of skin and laid the knife against it. The man jerked away, causing Long Rider to lose his hold. "Wait!" the man shrieked, the last of his composure finally gone. "You won't do it! You know I wasn't even there!"

Long Rider started to reach out again, then hesitated. "What's your name?" he asked.

To the terror-stricken man, it was a totally unexpected question. But he was glad enough to answer. Anything to gain time. "Henrys," he said. "Jock Henrys. Look . . . you know it isn't really me you're after. It's Barnes. He's the one behind all this. He's the one you want."

He was talking quickly, desperately. Long Rider pretended to hesitate, as if it would be a terrible disappointment to forgo even one moment of the torture he'd prepared himself for, the revenge he'd been savoring. The paint helped, of course, and the connection in most people's mind between Indians and savagery. "Maybe," he said. "But where can I find Barnes?"

Sensing possible salvation, at the very least a quick death, Henrys answered immediately. "He's got a ranch up in the foothills. Hell, more like a fort. Got lots of men there, maybe a dozen, and I'll tell you now . . . they ain't your average cowpokes."

Rapping out questions, Long Rider got Henrys to describe the route to the ranch, its layout, and as much of its routine as Henrys knew. By now, Henrys's initial fear was beginning to diminish a little.

"You say he has lots of men," Long Rider asked. "Hard men?"

Henrys started to nod.

"Men like you," Long Rider added softly.

Henrys flushed. Long Rider knew he would not get much more from him now. He picked up the knife again. Henrys flinched, ready to crawl, to beg. The knife blade flashed in the early morning sun . . . as Long Rider cut the cords tying Henrys's arms and legs to the stakes.

Henrys seemed confused for a moment. He rubbed his wrists. Long Rider pointed to the packhorse. "Mount," he ordered. "Ride to Barnes. Tell him I'm coming. Tell him he's a dead man."

Henrys got gingerly to his feet, as if he expected it was only a trick, and that in another moment this maniac would really be peeling off his skin, strip by strip, as he'd promised. But Long Rider, now with a pistol in his hand, made no move to stop him. Henrys mounted, wincing as his pelvis made contact with the packsaddle. But, when no shot came, he tugged on the reins, pulling the animal's head around. He dug in his heels, and the packhorse, grunting, started to trot away.

No bullets came after Henrys, as he'd half-expected. But words did, the painted killer's voice, floating after him. "Remember . . . tell Barnes I'm coming. Tell him he's a dead man."

# CHAPTER EIGHTEEN

As Henrys had told him, it was a big ranch, and there were a lot of men. But if personal safety had been Barnes's reason for choosing this particular location, his tactical sense was poor. The ranch was surrounded by hills and broken ground, good cover for an intruder.

After Long Rider had let Henrys go, he'd followed him, keeping well out of sight. Henrys had ridden as if the whole Apache Nation was on his tail. He'd gone straight to the ranch. Seeing buildings ahead, Long Rider took cover in a stand of trees while he studied the situation. Through his binoculars, he watched Henrys ride into the ranch yard, hell for leather, and leap from his horse. Long Rider was too far away to make out any words, but he could hear distant shouting. A moment later a man came out of the main house. Long Rider was pretty sure it was Barnes, although he was too far away to be positive. Whoever it was, shortly thereafter armed men were posted at all the approaches to the ranch.

Satisfied that he was now very close to his quarry, Long Rider rode back into the hills. Tonight, he would start his preparation. After an initial reconnaissance, he decided to station himself on a rugged ridge that overlooked the ranch buildings from only three hundred yards away.

He moved in slowly, two hours before first light. He'd left his horse tied nearly a mile back, in a small, hidden draw, then he'd come the rest of the way on foot, carrying his Sharps. By the time the sky began to lighten, he was in position, hidden among rocks and brush near the edge of the ridge. He liked high ground.

He studied the ranch all day, sometimes through his binoculars, when he was certain that the sun would not reflect from their lenses and give him away. He counted at least fourteen men, although there was so much coming and going that an exact count was difficult. Barnes came out of the main house a little before ten in the morning. Long Rider studied him carefully. It was difficult to make out his features, but his movements seemed nervous, tense. Undoubtedly he'd expected some trouble from Don Andres, otherwise, why all the men? But now, with Jock Henrys riding in, telling him that Jed and his men were dead and a crazy renegade was after him, Barnes was clearly shaken.

Long Rider considered shooting Barnes from the ridge top. With the Sharps, it would not be a particularly difficult shot. However, he resisted the temptation. He wanted Barnes to live with the knowledge that death was stalking him. He wanted every day to be an agony for the man who'd caused Mercedes's death. And when he finally killed him, he wanted Barnes to see that death had a face. Long Rider's.

But, to meet Barnes face-to-face it would be necessary to get his guards out of the way. That might not be too difficult. From his observations, Long Rider had reached the opinion they were typical hired gunmen—steady enough when the pay outweighed the risk, but quick to get the hell out when their work became too dangerous.

He'd slowly been formulating a plan to ruin morale among the gunmen. He had to first find a way to move into the ranch area in person. If there'd been nothing to worry about except the gunmen, that might not have been too difficult. By his third day of observations, Long Rider had noticed that they were growing bored. Their alertness was slowly slipping.

The main problem was a dog, a large black mongrel, a mean animal, and a constant barker. If anything moved near the ranch, even a squirrel running from hole to hole a hundred yards away, the dog went wild, barking, snarling, rushing in that direction. Any attempt Long Rider might make to steal into the ranch yard would immediately be given away by the dog.

A little after noon of the third day, this particular obstacle was removed. One of the men came out of a bunkhouse, walking too fast to suit the dog, and it began to bark, snarl, and lunge. The man snarled back, which made the dog snap at his leg. The man, cursing, drew his pistol and shot the dog dead.

The shot brought men running from every direction. A loud argument broke out between the man who'd shot the dog and another man who had valued the animal for its sentry abilities. But no one really cared about the dog. These were not kindly men. But then, the dog had not been very nice, either.

Now, Long Rider was free to make his next move, the first step in demoralizing Barnes's guards. He knew he'd have to act quickly; any day Barnes might grow tired of holing up in this rather desolate place and head for town. He might be easier to reach in town, but Long Rider wanted him right here, isolated, nervous, frightened, paranoid.

Returning to his horse and gear, Long Rider took a pad of paper and an indelible pencil from his saddlebags, then sat down and began to write. Within a few minutes he'd finished and sat looking at his work, satisfied. His next move would be to deliver the note he'd written. Which promised to be just a bit more dangerous than the writing itself.

He was back on his ridge top just as dusk began to fall. He studied the scene below with special care, fixing in his mind where every guard was posted. Dark fell quickly; it was a cloudy night. There was no moon; the darkness was intense.

Long Rider left the ridge about midnight, working his way downhill toward a small streambed. Over the years, the little stream had cut a small but deep gully that ran through the center of the ranch yard, a sunken highway that led straight into the enemy's camp. True, they'd posted a guard near the gully, but Long Rider had noticed that the man on duty tonight had a tendency to fall asleep when he was sure no one was watching.

Stopping next to the stream, Long Rider took off all his weapons, anything that might clink or slow him down. Except for his knife; he'd take that. Then after he'd scooped up mud to darken his face and hands, he began to work his way in toward the ranch, quickly at first, but as he neared the yard, more and more slowly, until, at the end, he was crawling with infinite care.

He could tell when he passed the guard near the gully; he could hear his soft snoring. When he was sure he'd penetrated far enough, Long Rider rolled out of the gully onto flat ground and immediately hid himself behind an outbuilding. Good. The bunkhouse was only a few yards away.

Moving in short rushes, he flattened himself against the bunkhouse's side wall. Now . . . around to the door. . . .

The sound of footsteps made him freeze. He pressed himself against the wall again, fighting to control his breathing. Two men, maybe more. If they came around to this side of the building . . .

Long Rider let his hand fall to the handle of his knife. His only hope was to surprise them when they came around the corner, cut them badly, then run for the gully.

But the men stopped at the bunkhouse's front corner. A match flared, lighting up a pair of hard-looking faces. There were two of them, one lighting a cigarette. "Hey, Jack," the other man said. "Henrys gets kinda worried about us smokin' on guard duty. He says it gives away our positions."

The man who'd been called Jack spit on the ground in disgust. "Hell, Henrys worries about too damn much. Nervous bastard. Probably a bedwetter." He chuckled. "Shit, Pete, remember when he come ridin' into the yard the other day, no gun on him, shirt cut to ribbons, babblin' 'bout some renegade wantin' to skin him alive?"

Now Pete chuckled, too. "Yeah. White as a sheet an' shakin' all over."

"Not half as bad as Barnes was shakin'. Thought he was gonna shit his britches when he heard about that renegade an' what he said. Good ol' Barnes, just standin' there shakin' an' cursin' Jed for killing that Mex bitch."

From the cigarette glow, Long Rider could see Pete shaking his head. "Wasn't respectful of Jed an' the others, them bein' dead an' all. Say, you suppose that hombre did kill all six of 'em by hisself?"

Jack grunted. "Doubt it. More likely, those Mexes hit 'em when they was drunk. Guess they were pretty worked up over the killins. Stupid o' Jed. . . ."

Pete spat disgustedly. "Ah, hell, so they shot some Mex bitch and her brother. What's another woman, more or less?"

Jack chuckled. "Depends on how long since you had one, don't it? But Mexicans an' Injuns? Well, whatta they count? Why, I remember the time me an' old Toby Thompson got us hold o' this Cheyenne girl . . . you remember Toby, doncha?"

"Yeah. Old Toby. Always good for a laugh."

"Well . . . we caught us this Cheyenne girl. Kinda pretty an' real young, maybe sixteen or seventeen, although it's kinda hard to tell how old they are, ain't it? Whatever, we had us some fun with her. She bit an' scratched at first, but Toby kinda cold-cocked her, an' we gave it to that little squaw but good."

Jack took another drag on his cigarette. "Bitch bit me, though, toward the end. So I got out my knife an' showed her a little fancy blade work. She sure as hell weren't much to look at after I finished."

"That's real nice, Jack. But Jesus, I gotta pee." Pete was fumbling with his trousers.

"Well, hell, don't go pissin' here, right in front o' the bunkhouse door," Jack said in disgust. "Head out a ways."

"Ah," Pete muttered. "You're a little old lady. Just like Henrys and Barnes."

Nevertheless, he walked away, disappearing into the dark, leaving Jack alone. As he watched the man, Long Rider felt a great anger growing inside himself, almost as great as the anger he'd felt when he saw Mercedes lying dead in the road.

Jack turned partly away. Long Rider was on him in an instant, his left hand going over Jack's mouth, his right hand driving the point of his knife deep into Jack's right kidney.

Jack shuddered, his body stiffening, the agony of the knife in his kidney too great to permit him to cry out or to struggle with his assailant. As Jack began to slump, Long Rider pulled the man's head back with his left hand, raised the knife, and slashed his exposed throat.

He did not let Jack fall, but dragged his twitching body near the bunkhouse's front door. He'd noticed a big hook close to the doorway for hanging saddles, harness, and other gear. Grunting with the effort, he hoisted Jack into the air and snagged his jacket on the hook, so that Jack was hanging against the front bunkhouse wall, only a couple of feet from the door, with his heels swinging several inches off the ground.

Long Rider could hear Pete whistling quietly to himself about thirty yards away while he watered the yard. At any moment he would come back. Long Rider was going to have to move fast.

He took the note he'd written from his pocket. Jack was wearing a knife in a sheath at his side. Long Rider pulled out the knife, held the note against Jack's chest, where the blood had not spread too thickly, then pinned it in place by driving the knife to the hilt in Jack's flesh.

Time to leave. He could hear Pete coming back, muttering to himself about how dark it was. But not too dark for him to make out Jack's body, hanging from the hook, next to the bunkhouse door. "Jesus Christ!" Long Rider heard him bellow, but by that time he was back in the gully, nearing the edge of the ranch yard.

He stopped where he had left his guns. As he rearmed himself, he could hear shouting and cursing from the ranch yard. Lanterns were being lit. Good. That would help them read the note he'd left. A note that would strike them even more strongly now, considering where he had left it. The note itself was quite simple. Written in large block letters, it read:

HENRY BARNES MUST DIE.
ANYONE PROTECTING BARNES WILL DIE WITH HIM.
LEAVE WHILE YOU HAVE THE CHANCE.


LONG RIDER

When the uproar behind him fell silent for a moment, Long Rider suspected they must be reading the note. He was sure of it when puzzled, angry shouting broke out, a general bedlam that grudgingly gave way to more organized yelling, just a voice or two now, giving orders, then giving them again. Apparently no one wanted to obey those orders. No one wanted to go out into the darkness and confront the man who had laughed at ranch security and who had butchered one of Barnes's hired killers just a few yards from where the rest were sleeping.

Long Rider walked further away from the ranch, moving up the streambed for a while, knowing he was leaving clear tracks behind him. He wanted to leave tracks.

When he got back to his horse, he mounted and rode away, once again doing nothing to cover his tracks. An hour later, he stopped on high ground and, without making camp, lay down with his bedroll over him and slept for several hours.

He was up at first light, eating out of a can of cold beans, looking from time to time over his back trail. He could see a long way, see almost to the ranch. He was not at all surprised when, about an hour after dawn, a distant line of horsemen showed far away, breasting a high point. They were coming after him.

Long Rider took time remounting, first checking his horse to make certain that there were no physical or equipment difficulties that might surprise him later. For the next day or two he would be counting on the condition of his horse. His life would depend on it.

All that day he rode steadily, staying just ahead of his pursuers. Apparently either Barnes or Henrys still had enough authority over their ragtag bunch of hired killers to get them to leave the comfort of the ranch and risk their necks. Or maybe they were simply angry over Jack's death, the humiliation of it. Now was the time to discover just how much discouragement they could take.

Long Rider varied his tactics, sometimes working hard to cover his trail, not so much to lose the men after him, but to make them struggle to follow. To tire them out. Each time they seemed about to give up, he would show himself on a distant ridge, a half-glimpsed figure wearing a long black leather coat with the image of a bird painted across the back, and the chase would be on again.

The second night, he made certain that he got his rest; he'd obscured his trail fairly well just before dark. They'd be unable to follow him through the night. Or so he hoped.

Sure enough, it was two hours after dawn before he spotted them again, more than a mile back, puzzling over his faint trail. He showed himself again, almost smiling as he imagined the tired cursing of the men behind him. They must be getting pretty sick of the whole damned thing.

He led them on through most of the day. Finally, about an hour before dark, he reached an area that would suit his purpose. The ground rose sheer ahead of him, with only a narrow track leading upward to the top of a low plateau. For a while he wondered if he hadn't outsmarted himself; his horse barely made it up the trail. If they caught up to him now . . .

But they were still over a mile behind. By the time they came into view, Long Rider had reached the top of the plateau and dismounted. He staked his horse out about twenty yards back, well away from the edge, invisible from below. Then he untied his bedroll and laid it near the edge of the precipice. Finally, he went back for his Sharps. As he settled down onto the ground, he saw that his pursuers were now about half a mile away.

Plenty of time. He lay on his belly and placed the carbine's forearm on top of the bedroll. He settled the stock against his shoulder and trial-sighted. Good. A steady position. And he could see for a long way.

He decided that he would open fire as soon as the riders were within five hundred yards, so he raised the rear sight and moved the crossbar into the five hundred yard position.

Closer and closer. Seven hundred yards, six hundred. Long Rider began to sight on the first rider's horse. Since it was coming straight at him, it was not an easy shot, but he took his time, first cranking back the big hammer, then slowing his breathing, half-collapsing over the Sharps, so that muscular tension would not make him shake, ruining his aim.

Five hundred yards. Pressure on the trigger. The butt slammed his shoulder as he fired, white smoke billowing out ahead of the muzzle, then, seemingly a long time later, a horse went down in a heap, its rider barely having time to jump clear.

Speed now, speed was important. Up with the breech, a little smoke escaping, another paper cartridge in place, down with the breech, the slight resistance as the back of the breech cut through the cartridge. He'd already placed several caps on a flat rock close at hand. He pressed one of the shiny copper caps in place, pulled the hammer all the way back, sighted, and fired again, the whole process taking about ten seconds.

Another horse went down. The riders were milling around in confusion, not sure at first where the shots were coming from, until they saw the big white balls of smoke rising from the cliff top. They would realize what a bad position they were in, out in the open, with a hidden marksman, untouchable, able to pick them off one by one if he decided to switch from killing horses to killing men. If they had any brains, they'd ride away as fast as they could, until they were out of range.

Two men decided to do just the opposite. Long Rider couldn't figure out if they thought that he might shoot them in the back if they ran or if they were just brave. They put spurs to their mounts and rushed straight toward him, straight toward the trail that led up the cliff.

That was bad. If they reached the shelter of the bluff below him, they could come up the trail on foot, hiding behind rocks and brush. He'd have to show himself to pick them off, then the others would have a good shot at him.

They were already within three hundred yards. Cover lay ahead, scattered boulders, and wrinkles in the flinty ground. If they got any closer . . .

Long Rider had not wanted to kill any of the men. Not if he could help it. Barnes was the one he was after. But now it was them or him.

He slid the sight's crossbar lower, aimed, fired. One man had almost made it to cover, but the Sharps's huge bullet plucked him from the saddle as if he'd run into an invisible tree limb.

The man behind him hesitated, pulled his horse to a stop, then decided to continue on. His slight hesitation gave Long Rider time to reload. Another bellow from the Sharps, and the man spun out of the saddle, half his right side blown away.

By now, the others were far away, nearly a half mile back, milling around in a tight, frustrated circle. They all saw the man they'd been chasing stand up on his cliff top, out of range. Long Rider stood watching them for nearly a full minute, then he turned and walked away, disappearing from view.

There was a heated discussion among the survivors. Some of the men, led by Henrys, wanted to continue after Long Rider. "He'll make a mistake sooner or later," Henrys insisted. "And then we'll have him."

"And how many more of us is he gonna kill before that happens?" another man snarled back. The two men glowered at one another for a few seconds. Henrys wanted Long Rider badly; the man had humiliated him. But, when he saw that the others were not about to follow him, he sullenly decided to go back with them. He did not want Long Rider quite badly enough to risk his neck alone.

Barnes's guardians, four of them mounted double, made camp that night still nearly half a day's ride from the ranch. The mood was not good. It improved considerably when several men produced bottles of whiskey and rum. A couple of the men wondered if it was a good idea to drink so much when they were on the trail of such a dangerous man, but eventually, disgusted, they too began to drink, figuring Long Rider was far gone by now.

By three in the morning, all of the men, including the two guards who'd been posted at the far limits of the light from the campfire, were lost in drunken slumber. None of them was aware of the half-naked figure crawling closer and closer to their camp.

It took Long Rider an hour to reach the center of the camp. Moving with agonizing slowness, he went from man to man, checking the breathing of each one to make certain he was deeply asleep. Then he draped something over each body. Finally, he wedged a piece of paper in between two rocks next to the campfire. Satisfied, he quickly moved away until he was lost in the darkness.

None of the men were feeling too well when they woke up the next morning; the whiskey and rum they had drunk had been low-grade rotgut. The first man to come out of his stupor automatically started to rub his hand over his face, but, as his hand rose, it picked up a piece of light rope, draped over his bedroll, and dragged it over his face. "What the . . . ?" the man growled, shaking the rope from his hand. "Who the hell . . . ?"

Then, as he sat up, he noticed that each of the other ten men remaining had a similar length of line draped over his blankets, near his throat. "Hey!" he shouted. "Hey! Wake up!"

Grumbling, the others awakened, many of them swearing as their hands snagged the pieces of line. Within thirty seconds, men were on their feet, confused, swearing, each thinking one of the others must have played a practical joke during the night.

Then one of them noticed the piece of paper wedged in between the two rocks. He snatched it up, and before he had even told the others what was written on it, they all knew. The words were the same as the words on the note that Long Rider had left pinned to Jack's dead body outside the bunkhouse door.

"Goddamn!" one of the men burst out. "That sneaky son of a bitch was right here in our camp!"

Another of the men, one who'd been slow getting up, looked down at the piece of line lying across his upper body. He shuddered. "He coulda cut our throats, easier'n pie," he mumbled.

All of them exploded into frantic motion, saddling horses, tying down gear. "He ain't human," one man said as he mounted. "I'm pullin' out, just like the note says."

"Wait a minute," Henrys replied angrily. "He's just a man. He can be beaten."

The mounted man glared back at Henrys. "Oh, yeah? You sure as hell had your chance with him an' you come runnin' back to the ranch with your tail tucked between your legs. Don't give me none o' your crap."

Henrys stood by his horse as the rest of the men mounted. They were in such a hurry that they left a coffeepot sitting next to the cold ashes of the campfire. Henrys stared back down the trail, silently cursing the man who'd made him crawl. Then, remembering the terrible eyes that had stared into his own, the coldness in them, their total lack of expression, he shuddered. Suddenly, he realized that he was standing all alone, with the others riding hard for the ranch. Casting a nervous look over his shoulder, he kicked the coffeepot, quickly mounted, and whipped his horse along after the others.

A quarter of a mile away, concealed in a patch of dwarf oak, Long Rider watched the riders, strung out in no particular order now, as they disappeared, one by one, around a bend in the trail. They were no longer his pursuers, but a group of cowed, fleeing fugitives.

# CHAPTER NINETEEN

The ranch was in an uproar. Cursing, kicking at unwanted gear, the gunmen were packing up. Barnes stood by the bunkhouse door, shouting at them. "You've got to stay!" he screamed. "I paid you!"

One of the men broke off packing his saddlebags and walked out the door to stand directly in front of Barnes. Nose to nose. Barnes shrank back a little; the man's breath stank horribly. His eyes were wild. "You didn't pay enough," the gunman snarled. "Not enough to die for. You said all we'd have to do is scare a few Mex'kins. Not get picked off, one by one, by some kinda invisible spook who might just show up in the outhouse when a man wants to take a shit. Naw, Barnes, you didn't tell us nearly enough. So keep outta our way, or you'll end up gettin' a hell of a lot more'n you paid for."

The man turned on his heel and walked back into the bunkhouse. Barnes had an overwhelming desire to shoot him in the back. But he knew that the man's friends would then simply shoot him.

He spun away from the bunkhouse, then walked, stiff-legged, back to the main house. He was seething inside. And scared. That long-haired bastard who'd teamed up with the old Spaniard had proven to be bad news from the word go. And now he was after Barnes personally. Because of some damned señorita.

When he'd first heard that his guards were leaving, Barnes had immediately thought of returning with them to Los Angeles. But what good would that do? He had a feeling that even if he locked himself up inside an impregnable castle for a year, the day he walked out, that bastard, who now seemed to be calling himself some silly Indian name . . . what was it? Long Rider? The day he stepped out into the open air, even if it was five years from now, Long Rider would be waiting for him.

This whole damned mess would have to be taken care of today, or he'd be looking over his shoulder for the rest of his life. Which would probably be short. The bastard was good. Incredibly good.

The problem was, they'd been meeting him head-on. Maybe it was time to start using brains instead of idiot gunhands. Set a trap. Although Barnes was scared—who wouldn't be?—he was not a coward. He'd have to end this thing now, one way or the other.

When he walked into the house, he heard sounds from down a hallway. That must be Henrys, packing to hightail it out, just like the others. He'd let Henrys stay in a spare room in the main house, so someone would be close to him at all times, in case Long Rider got past the guards and into the house itself.

Henrys. Now there was a man who had a bone to pick with Long Rider. Maybe more than one bone. And Barnes knew that Henrys was a greedy man.

He walked down the hall, stood in the doorway to Henrys's room. Henrys was just about finished packing, but looked up when he saw Barnes. "It's over, Barnes. I'm goin'," the gunman said sullenly. "Don't try to stop me."

Barnes shrugged. "I won't try. But money might. And revenge."

Henrys turned again. "What the hell do you mean?"

"It's simple. That man can be had. Any man can. You just gotta use your head."

"Yeah, yeah, I s'pose you're right. That's what I tried to tell the others. But we sure ain't got the better of him yet."

"I think I know a way," Barnes said. He could see that Henrys was beginning to pay a little more attention. "I've got a thousand dollars for you. If you help me bushwhack that bastard."

By now, Henrys had suspended his packing, but he still looked dubious. Barnes quickly followed up. "I know he's out there somewhere, watching. He'll see the men leave. He'll also see me stay behind, and he'll see me go into the house with a rifle. He'll come on in after me. But what he won't see is the other man, the one who stayed behind, the one hiding out in the barn, with a shotgun. Want to guess who that man'll be?"

Henrys looked tempted for a moment, then he slowly turned back to his packing. "Naw," he muttered. "Too risky."

"Two thousand dollars," Barnes said curtly. Henrys did not turn around. "Three thousand."

Henrys slowly straightened up from his packing. Three thousand dollars. That was a lot of money. More than three years pay for the average cowhand. Three thousand dollars would buy a lot of whiskey, a lot of women, and a lot of comfort. "Well," he said hesitantly. "Maybe."

Long Rider was back on his ridge top, observing the wild activity below him. Men were saddling horses, packing gear, obviously getting ready to ride out. He wondered if Barnes would ride out with them. They probably wouldn't let him; he'd become their albatross.

The men left in a compact body that bristled with guns. They weren't taking any chances. He watched them leave the ranch yard. He counted them carefully. Two more than the number of men who'd ridden back from the chase. They must have been guards left behind to protect Barnes, while the others had been out scouring the countryside.

He saw a man come out onto the ranch house's front porch. The man was carrying a rifle. He shouted something after the departing gunmen. Long Rider raised his binoculars. It was Barnes. It had worked. He was alone now.

Barnes stood on the porch for another five minutes, until the dust churned up by all the departing horses had died down. Then, still carrying the rifle, he went back inside.

Long Rider carefully swept the yard with his binoculars. Not a sign of life. Except for a saddled horse tied near the back of the house. He'd seen Barnes saddle it while the men were getting ready to leave. He must be planning on riding out on his own. Or maybe he just wanted it there for a quick escape.

Long Rider waited another half hour, to make sure that it was not a trick, that the guards would not come riding back into the yard the moment he made his move. Finally, he saw them disappearing over a hill about three miles away, a line of tiny figures.

Time to go in now. Time to end it all. Time to wipe away Henry Barnes. Time for vengeance.

But, as Long Rider walked back down the ridge toward his horse, something was niggling at the back of his mind. He had mounted and was partway to the ranch when he finally figured out what it was. Henry Barnes had never shown much love for going it on his own, man-to-man. It was doubtful he'd changed now. No, there was some kind of surprise waiting in that ranch yard.

Inside the ranch house, Barnes went from window to window, looking for signs of his approaching enemy. He knew that he would come. He knew that within a short time either he'd be dead or that damned renegade would be dead.

He went into the house's main room and stopped just inside the front door, out of sight. The barn where Henrys was hidden was only about thirty yards away. "You staying awake in there?" he hissed.

"Yeah," Henrys's voice came back. "You see anything yet?"

"No. I'll tell you when I do. I'll yell out for the bastard to come and get me. He'll probably move right past where you're hiding."

A grunt from Henrys. Barnes went back into the house, began keeping lookout from the windows again. There were not many, and most of them were near the front of the house. If Long Rider came after him, that's the way he'd have to come; the only side window looked out over open ground. No cover there. By God, maybe they'd get him after all!

And if not, maybe he'd live to laugh another day. Henrys didn't know about the saddled horse he'd tied up in the back of the house. Maybe if Long Rider and Henrys got into a fight, he'd just skedaddle, ride on out and let them finish one another off. That ten-gauge scatter-gun of Henrys's would make mincemeat out of anything that got close enough.

Nothing to do but settle down and wait. Keep a sharp lookout. Goddamn hard on the nerves, though. And all because of that old bastard, Andres Velasquez, and his antique ranch. Good land, of course, but Barnes knew he could have lived without it. The trouble was, accumulating land, grabbing for power, had become an addiction. He did not like it when someone resisted, fouled up his plans. If he lived through this, he'd make the old man pay.

There! About five hundred yards away. A rider approaching!

It was him, all right; no mistaking that long black coat he'd taken to wearing. Or that long hair. Riding straight on in, bold as brass.

Barnes ran to the front door, keeping out of sight. "He's coming!" he hissed to Henrys. "Oughta be right in front of you in four or five minutes."

"I'll get him," Henrys promised.

Barnes ran back to the window, wondering how much closer Long Rider had gotten. Where the hell was he? No sign of anyone at all! The bastard had simply disappeared into thin air!

Long Rider had disappeared all right, but only from Barnes's view. He'd seen a shadow move behind one of the house's windows. He'd been spotted, as he'd planned. Now, using the roughness of the ground around the ranch, he simply guided his horse into a depression in the terrain deep enough to screen him from the house. Out of sight, he slipped off his horse's back.

From here, he'd go in on foot. Carefully. He drew his Winchester from its saddle scabbard, then, bent low, he began to move slowly toward the ranch buildings, his eyes searching the terrain ahead, looking for anything, natural or man-made, that would further screen his approach.

Finally, he was in the ranch yard itself, hidden behind the bunkhouse. Not a sound anywhere. Yet, the silence screamed with menace. Instinctively, Long Rider settled down to wait. Years as a hunter had taught him how to wait very patiently.

But Henry Barnes had never been a hunter, and the terrible silence out in the yard was destroying his nerves. Where was the bastard? Had he only imagined he'd seen him? Of course not. The rider he'd spotted had been real enough. He wasn't losing his mind.

Finally, he could stand the waiting no longer. "Henrys," he called out softly. "You see anything?"

"Uh-uh. Now shut the hell up!"

But it was too late. Long Rider had heard the interchange, had heard Henrys's voice coming from the barn. He'd even been able to pinpoint Henrys's location within the barn. Next to a small door.

The barn was old, made of thin, flimsy, rotting planks. Long Rider stepped out from behind the bunkhouse. Firing his Winchester from the hip, he poured a dozen rounds into the side of the barn, just to the left of the little door.

Dust and rotting wood chips flew from the side of the old structure, while the roar of gunfire bounced back off the surrounding hills. Long Rider stepped back a pace, half hidden by the bunkhouse wall again, waiting. There was a pause of a few seconds, then a slow-moving figure staggered out of the barn door. Henrys, shot to pieces, with at least half of the rounds Long Rider had fired having found his body.

"You . . . son of a bitch," Henrys croaked in a grating, pain-choked voice. "You . . ."

He was carrying a shotgun. He tried to raise it to fire at Long Rider, but it appeared to be a much heavier weight than he could manage. He took another shambling step forward. The twin muzzles of the shotgun were pointing down at the ground. "You . . ." he managed to say again. Then the shotgun went off, kicking up clods of dirt a yard ahead of Henrys. The gun's recoil destroyed the rest of Henrys's balance. He fell onto his side, the shotgun slipping from dying fingers.

Long Rider started to step out from behind the bunkhouse, but a scream of rage and fear from the main house stopped him. "Bastard!" Barnes was screaming. "Son of a bitch!"

Barnes opened fire with his Winchester, but his hands were shaking so badly that all his shots missed. Long Rider returned the fire. Some of his bullets chipped wood from the house's door frame, but by then Barnes had ducked back inside.

Rush the house? Maybe Barnes was waiting for him to do just that. Then, when he had no cover, Barnes would open up again with the rifle.

There was a sudden sound of breaking glass from the back of the house, a grunt of pain, then, a moment later, a desperate cry, followed by the pounding of hooves. Damn! Barnes had run to that horse Long Rider had seen from the ridge top, the one tied up at the rear of the house. He was making a run for it!

No time for caution now. Long Rider raced back across the ranch yard, toward the place where he'd left his horse. Reaching it, he vaulted into the saddle, then pulled his mount around and rammed his heels into its side. A mistake, because the sudden pain made the big black rear up on its hind legs, which cost time.

But it also gave Long Rider time to think. There was only one way Barnes could have gone, considering the terrain. Hills and gullies would force him to ride in an arc. And from where Long Rider was now sitting, he could cut him off.

With the black now under control, Long Rider raced off to the side, cutting around a big gully. Sure enough, there, only a hundred yards ahead, Barnes came racing around the corner of a hill, flat out on his horse, riding hell for leather.

Long Rider set off in pursuit. He saw Barnes turn in the saddle, look back at him. Barnes was still carrying the rifle. He held it behind him with one hand, squeezed off a shot. The bullet came nowhere near Long Rider, but Barnes, turning, had temporarily lost control of his horse. The animal stumbled, recovered. The sudden shock caused Barnes to lose his hold on the rifle. It fell to the ground. Long Rider could see no pistol. Barnes now seemed to be totally unarmed.

It had boiled down to a matter of horseflesh. And Long Rider had the better horse. The big black stallion quickly gained on Barnes's laboring mount. Within minutes, Long Rider had gotten close enough to blow Barnes out of the saddle . . . if that's what he wanted to do. No. Too easy that way.

Then Long Rider remembered his reata. The one Jorge had given him. It lay tied to the saddle near his right hand.

Long Rider freed the reata, shook out a loop. He might not be as good with it as Don Andres's vaqueros, but they'd taught him a great deal.

He was now only about ten yards behind Barnes. He began to whirl the rawhide loop around his head. He stood in the stirrups and threw.

The loop settled over Barnes's head. Long Rider pulled back, tightening the loop before it could slip lower. The thin rawhide bit into Barnes's neck. Long Rider saw him raise a hand, paw at the noose around his neck, but by then Long Rider was jerking backward on the reata. Barnes fell over the back of his horse. He hit the ground hard, and for a few seconds he lay stunned, with the reata still around his neck.

There was a large tree to one side of the trail. Long Rider used those few seconds to throw his end of the reata over a limb that jutted out ten feet above the trail. Then he snubbed the reata to his saddle horn and began to back his horse away.

The noose jerked Barnes to his feet, then began to slowly haul him into the air. Barnes was regaining his senses now; he was horribly aware of what was happening. He pawed at the noose. It was tightening around his neck, cutting into his flesh, but he could not fight the strength of Long Rider's horse. Within seconds he was hanging by his neck from the limb, his feet several inches off the ground.

Long Rider quickly tied his end of the reata to another tree, then he quietly sat his horse several yards away to watch Barnes slowly strangle. It took a long time. Barnes, in an effort to save his life, stopped fighting the noose around his neck and tried to climb the reata, hand over hand, hoping to reach the tree limb above.

But he lacked the strength. He hung for several seconds, arm muscles straining, eyes desperate. Then he fell, the loop tightening again, biting into his neck.

Long Rider continued to watch him struggle, watched Henry Barnes's legs kick at the air, saw his face slowly turn purple, his eyes bulge, his tongue protrude from his mouth. Long Rider was sickened. He thought about drawing his pistol and putting Barnes out of his misery. Then he remembered Mercedes, lying in the dust of that lonely road, her dreams shattered by Jed's bullet. That beautiful young woman, destroyed, ultimately by the greed of the man who was slowly strangling in front of him. Wasn't hanging the White Man's way of justice?

Long Rider's hand moved away from the butt of his pistol. He took one last look into Barnes's terrified eyes, then turned his horse and rode away. He twisted in the saddle once and looked back. Barnes was no longer moving. He hung slackly, his head twisted over at an acute angle. Long Rider noticed that Barnes had fouled his pants.

He kept riding until he began to realize he did not know in which of the four directions to ride. Even as he realized this, images came into his mind of what lay to the south. El Rancho de Las Palomas. A broad, beautiful valley. A community of people among whom he now had a place. A home. Instinctively, his fingers tightened on the reins, ready to send his horse in that direction.

Then other images filled his mind. Mercedes's beautiful face, the way it had shone with light each time they made love. An image of Jorge, smiling, laughing, full of life.

Except that Mercedes and Jorge were no longer full of life. They were both dead. Too many people were dead, too much had been lost. For Long Rider, El Rancho de Las Palomas was a snakepit of memories. Painful memories.

It took him a while, then he remembered what he had realized when he'd left the People, his own Oglala. That there never was any going back. Only going forward, perhaps into emptiness, perhaps into aloneness, but . . . going.

He pulled his horse's head around, toward the north. He smiled bitterly. It looked like he would be seeing winter after all.

A special offer for people who enjoy reading the best Westerns published today.

# WESTERNS!

## NO OBLIGATION

### Mail the coupon below

To start your subscription and receive 2 FREE WESTERNS, fill out the coupon below and mail it today. We'll send your first shipment which includes 2 FREE BOOKS as soon as we receive it.

---

Mail To: **True Value Home Subscription Services, Inc. P.O. Box 5235
120 Brighton Road, Clifton, New Jersey 07015-5235**

YES! I want to start reviewing the very best Westerns being published today. Send me my first shipment of 6 Westerns for me to preview FREE for 10 days. If I decide to keep them, I'll pay for just 4 of the books at the low subscriber price of $2.75 each; a total $11.00 (a $21.00 value). Then each month I'll receive the 6 newest and best Westerns to preview Free for 10 days. If I'm not satisfied I may return them within 10 days and owe nothing. Otherwise I'll be billed at the special low subscriber rate of $2.75 each; a total of $16.50 (at least a $21.00 value) and save $4.50 off the publishers price. There are never any shipping, handling or other hidden charges. I understand I am under no obligation to purchase any number of books and I can cancel my subscription at any time, no questions asked. In any case the 2 FREE books are mine to keep.

Name _____

Street Address _____ Apt. No. _____

City _____ State _____ Zip Code _____

Telephone _____

Signature _____
(if under 18 parent or guardian must sign)                    831

Terms and prices subject to change. Orders subject
to acceptance by True Value Home Subscription
Services, Inc.